Critical Praise for *Ar*

*Winner of the California Boo

"Greer does a superb job of transcending conventional genrefication, bringing something fresh to contemporary literature . . . A very enjoyable read [with a] highly inventive structure, full of eccentricities and rock music factoids."

—Library Journal

"Ambitious and intriguing . . . Strong writing and shrewd perceptions prevail, backed by wry humor, compelling stumblebum characters, and arresting insights into the dream of art."

—Booklist

"Greer's prose shines [with] moments where the writing becomes urgent and truly moving. This is the way the real and the invented Kurt [Cobain] would have wanted it."

—Los Angeles Times Book Review

"*Artificial Light* mixes genres for a complex and rewarding head scratch. It's a love letter to an unlovable city relayed in prose that is fluid with depth and reverberation."

—Eye Weekly (Toronto, Canada)

"Greer is drunk on words and uses this altered state like a hit man with a zip gun, delivering a scattering of one poetic paragraph after another . . . At times he comes on like a late-night booze hound, purging his drunken philosophies and theories in haphazard but engaging fashion . . . He is enthralling, slightly buzzed tippler of poetic phrases and brilliant insights."

—Dayton Daily News

"Big-ambition fiction . . . Carries a whiff of classic Bret Easton Ellis."

—Time Out New York

"*Artificial Light* is an ambitious . . . and deliberately perplexing novel about love; of rock 'n' roll, of substance abuse, of late-night bars, of language, of what or whoever is inaccessible."

—*Magnet*

"Greer concocts his story in a refreshing way that makes it difficult not to get lost in this wonderful tangle of a story that's punctuated by hauntingly beautiful prose."

—*Chart* (Canada)

"When is flight not-flight? How does a dead (very dead) celebrity manage to be not-dead? Why are Dayton, Ohio, and not-Dayton so endgame-compatible? James Greer eats being and non-being for breakfast, and his tale is one of Parmenidian oompah and shebang. As apocalyptic page-turners go, *Artificial Light* beats the bejeezus out of the last dozen Thomas Pynchons, the last nineteen Don DeLillos, and the last forty-three Kurt Vonneguts. I wouldn't shit ya."

—Richard Meltzer, author of *A Whore Just Like the Rest*

"Fiat Lux gleams like an onyx from a vivid and darkly mythical world. She is impossible to forget and her skewed cynicism and solipsistic melancholy linger long after you've turned the final page. Greer's writing is lean and poetic, shot through with sagacious observations and demented humor, but at the heart of his strange semi–sci fi world there is a huge human tenderness, moments of heart-rending lyrical beauty, and a rabid breathtaking imagination."

—Helen Walsh, author of *Brass*

"*Artificial Light* skates on the purity of confession. It's a brutal reveal; an Abyss Narrative with hooks. Read it in a rush of abomination and rise above, rise above."

—Stephen Malkmus

THE
FAILURE

THE
FAILURE

BY

JAMES GREER

AKASHIC BOOKS
NEW YORK

Published by Akashic Books
©2010 James Greer

ISBN-13: 978-1-933354-97-2
Library of Congress Control Number: 2009922939

First printing
Printed in Canada

Akashic Books
PO Box 1456
New York, NY 10009
info@akashicbooks.com
www.akashicbooks.com

To W.W.

ACKNOWLEDGMENTS

This book would not have been written, much less published, without the inspiration and support of Stephanie Sayers. Thanks also to Tad Floridis at Canongate for the title and general editorial guidance. Everyone at Akashic—Johnny Temple, Johanna Ingalls, and especially Aaron Petrovich—has been from first to last both supportive and helpful to an unreasonable degree. Thanks to Dennis Cooper, for his initial belief in my writing and continued encouragement. To Robert Pollard for the power of suck, etc. To Steven Soderbergh for screwing up my life in exactly the right measure. To Randy Howze for listening. Finally, a general thanks to everyone who has managed to put up with my self-absorbed, ill-humored, and monkish habits, allowing me to write the only way I know how: stony-hearted and alone.

The failure is unaware of himself as a failure.
To fail at failure—even to be aware of having failed—
could be construed as a kind of success.
—G. M. Holliston, *The Science of Fear*

1. HOW GUY FORGET
ENDED UP IN A COMA

G uy Forget—careening across Larkin Heights in a
stolen Mini Cooper—suffused with bloodlust and
baring a grin full of teeth, failed to hear the polyphonic bell-
ing of his cell phone. This was a mistake, for two reasons.

Had he heard his phone, and answered the call, Guy
would have learned three things: that his wealthy, boorish
father had died of a heart attack; that his wealthy, boorish
father's will had provided Guy with exactly enough cash,
after taxes, to fund the prototype for Pandemonium; and
that his wealthy, boorish father had included in his will a
personal message for Guy to the effect that, despite their
differences, and their less-than-communicative relationship
over the years, Guy's wealthy, boorish father did, in his own
unspectacular way, love his second son.

Had he heard and answered his phone, Guy would
also have been distracted sufficiently from his murderous
thoughts to lay off the accelerator, and would therefore
have slowed down sufficiently to avoid the near-fatal collision

awaiting him around the fourth curve of the bendy road down which he was driving too fast.

Because he did not hear or answer his phone, Guy Forget was in a coma from which he was not expected to recover. His surviving relatives—his mother Laura, tense, brittle-framed, already shaken by the recent death of her husband, who, even though she hated him, represented a kind of vital force that helped make sense of her life; and his older brother Marcus, balding, self-absorbed professor of theoretical physics at M.I.T., whose adherence to the code of abstraction respected by all professors of theoretical physics everywhere extended to forgetting, from time to time, his wife Constance's existence—were divided on the question of whether to pull Guy's plug and end what remained of his corporeal viability, or, to be plain, of himself.

Laura was a seriously lapsed Roman Catholic who felt a distinct unease at ending Guy's life "without at least asking him," as she put it to Marcus over coffee at the hospital commissary in Los Angeles.

-Mom, he's in a coma. That's the whole sort of coma issue, replied Marcus, patiently. He was used to treating everyone, especially his mother, as if they were children, and needed to have even the most basic concepts explained simply.

-People come out of comas.

-Not people with Guy's level of brain activity. Or inactivity, more precisely. He's a vegetable. There's nothing about Guy that makes him human anymore.

-Mrs. Sanderson said that she read about this one . . .

-Mrs. Sanderson is not a doctor. *People* magazine is not, I'm pretty sure, a peer-reviewed medical journal.

-Those doctors don't get everything right. What about AIDS?

-What *about* AIDS?

-Well, they were wrong. It doesn't even exist.

-I'm sorry?

-It's like you live in a hole. You didn't hear about this?

-Mom, that's so utterly bizarre I'm going to refrain from comment.

-Saying that doesn't make it any less true.

-I suppose. In *crazy* world. Marcus reached across the table and wrapped his mother's tiny hands in his own, almost invisibly pale palms. -Whatever there was of Guy, his essence, has dispersed back into the universe. If it's any comfort, recent research has led some in the scientific community to believe that quantum consciousness exists independent of physical being—at very basic levels, on the Planck scale. In that sense—

-Marcus, interrupted Laura, I don't want to pull the plug. I just don't.

Marcus shrugged. -Okay. He looked at his watch. -I've still got time to catch the red-eye back to Boston. You staying, or . . .

-God, no.

2. INTRODUCTION OF THE VILLAIN
SVEN TRANSVOORT, UNDISCLOSED LOCATION, SEVERAL WEEKS AFTER THE KOREAN CHECK-CASHING FIASCO

———————————————

My name is Sven Transvoort. Obviously, that's not my real name, but it's the one everyone who knows me thinks is my real name. Reason: it's actually my real name. See? I lied! I do that a lot. I am an inherently trustworthy person. I am, in a word, villainous, and I don't have to explain myself to you, or anyone, because for all you know I may be one of Hegel's world-historical individuals who doesn't have to play by the rules. Like Napoleon. I have certain things in common with Napoleon. I'm not French, this much is true. Not a military strategist, or an army man of any sort. In fact, guns make me nervous. If guns didn't make me nervous, there would not be much to this story, in fact. Because guns make me nervous, I am forced instead to rely on my cunning. On my devious nature. On my villainy. I'm pretty sure Napoleon, from what I've read, possessed a certain devious streak. And there are, to this day, countries who consider him villainous.

Consider this my confession. I brought Guy down, you

see, I pricked his pretty bubble. I don't feel guilty—but I do feel that if I don't say something I won't get the credit I deserve, if I don't speak up. The squeaky wheel gets the credit, or something, right? Am I right?

Guy didn't know me as Sven Transvoort, of course. He knew me by that name, but not as Sven Transvoort the guy who'd sell his own sister down the river for a nickel, whatever that means. He knew me as someone he trusted, which is to say he didn't know me at all. What kind of a fool would trust me? I wear a T-shirt with the name of a punk rock band called Reasonable Sleep five or six days out of the week. I have wild, curly dark hair, thick-lensed glasses, and a gut you can hide things in. Seriously. You can tuck three grapefruits in my belly fat, no problem.

On the other hand, I might be dangerously thin, a consequence of my ongoing battle with prescription painkillers that has no effect whatsoever on my work, on the quality of my work. I could be a computer engineer student at Caltech, also an artist, and while we're at it a gallery owner. It's just a little gallery, really just one room in Chinatown, but my loft space downtown is pretty sumptuous. Certainly more so than you'd expect from a student/artist/small-time gallery owner. Or maybe I'm none of these things. Maybe I'm a private detective. Or a cop. Or a jewel thief. Or a product of Heidegger's "question of being," which both he and I believe to be the central question of our time, and may explain everything about what happened to Guy Forget. Or nothing.

I am, whoever I am, a dangerous character. I am the last person you would suspect. But I am the first person you should avoid. I hated Guy Forget with intensity, with white heat and black magic. I hated him from the moment

I laid eyes on him. I would have done anything to bring him down, and I did.

The fulfillment of a life's ambition is rarely so sweet as the anticipation of its fulfillment. I think that's a quote from the writer Fiat Lux, I don't know if you remember, the one who disappeared off the face of the earth a few years ago. Hardly anyone remembers her anymore.

What did Fiat Lux know? I used to wonder. I don't wonder anymore.

3. GUY AND HIS BEST FRIEND BILLY DRINKING IN A BAR LATE AT NIGHT, THREE DAYS BEFORE THE KOREAN CHECK-CASHING FIASCO

There's no dirt in this bar. It's very clean, said Guy.

-You say that like it's a bad thing, said his best friend of five years, Billy.

-It kind of is. You don't go to bars for hygiene.

-Well, no, obviously. But this is Los Angeles. Everything's clean.

-That's not true. There's a sheen of grit over the whole city, it gets into your pores even. I'll bet right now you have a body-dirt ratio of about nineteen percent.

-I took a shower before we came out.

-That's why it's so low. I didn't take a shower. My ratio's probably more like fifty-fifty.

-You're gross.

-Sure, blame the messenger.

Lucy, the bar maid, brought two pink drinks to the table, set them down, picking up the empties and the sodden napkins.

-Thanks, Lucy.

-Hey, Lucy, said Billy. -I got a new one. It's good.

Lucy rolled her eyes.

-Okay.

-Okay. Here goes. Hey, baby, your legs are so long I'd have to take a cab to kiss you.

-That's . . .

-*Taxi!*

-Sorry about the mess, said Guy, nodding toward the tangle of melted drink straws in the center of the table.

-Pretty, said Lucy.

-It's art! said Billy. -It's straw art. Bring us more straws so that we can express our feelings with straws.

-Can we pay for our drinks with straw art? asked Guy.

-Someday it might be valuable.

-Since when do you guys pay for drinks? said Lucy, walking away.

-She has a point, said Billy.

-Okay.

-You want to try reading minds on some girls?

-Not tonight. It's too much effort.

-How is that too much effort? Anything that involves girls is worthwhile. That's a direct quote from your brain.

-I never said that.

-I said from your brain. Maybe I can read your mind.

-There aren't even any girls.

-What bar are *you* in?

-Your standards are appallingly low.

-Yes.

Lucy came back over to the table with a handful of drink straws.

-You can have these, but no more melting them in the candle. It stinks up the whole place.

-Guy was just telling me it's too clean in here. Weren't you just telling me that, Guy?

-I was just telling Billy that.

-If Gregory comes in I'll get yelled at and you guys will get thrown out.

-I'll handle Gregory, said Billy. -He won't throw us out. He's got a crush on me.

-You wish, said Guy.

-Just . . . no melting, said Lucy.

She turned back to the bar.

-Without melting, there's really no point, said Billy, sadly.

-There's twisting and bending and fitting the end of one into the end of another, or the end of one into the other end of itself, creating a triangle, which can then be linked with other triangles.

-Yeah.

Guy drained his drink. The ice cubes clattered in his glass as he set it down.

-All right. I'll do mind reading. But only for one more drink. And you have to go get the girl.

Billy got up out of the banquette immediately, headed to a nearby table occupied by five drinking girls, where he pulled up a chair and engaged in a brief but intense conversation with an attractive young woman in a black dress. Her hair was dyed bright blond, and she made slits of her eyes as she listened to Billy.

Billy got up, shaking hands with the attractive woman before heading back to the banquette.

-She's good, he said, sliding into his seat.

-What's her name?

-Forgot to ask. Here she comes . . .

4. MARCUS, GUY'S BROTHER, CONTEMPLATES WHAT MIGHT HAVE BEEN, STANDING AT THE WINDOW OF HIS OFFICE IN CAMBRIDGE, THE SAME DAY AS THE KOREAN CHECK-CASHING FIASCO

Marcus sat at his desk in his office. From the window, he had a clear view of the River Charles, which legend tells used to freeze over regularly come winter, but Marcus had lived here nearly ten years and never seen it happen.

He stood up and went to the window. His breath condensed on the windowpane. *I was the shadow of the waxwing slain*, he thought.

Marcus sighed, and moved away. He avoided at all costs the blackboard on the far side of the office, avoided even looking in that direction, because the blackboard was almost empty. An empty blackboard is worse than a blackboard full of dead ends to a professor of quantum chromodynamics. An empty blackboard reflects an empty mind. It's like, what if someone came up and said, "Non-Abelian gauge theory is just a chimera, and I can prove it using the very same gauge invariant QCD Lagrangian in front of which you genuflect daily." How would I feel then? How would anyone feel? Empty.

What if I'd just given him the money when he asked? thought Marcus. I have the money. I have plenty of money.

Never wanted to be the sane one, the responsible one. How did that happen? All through childhood I was odd boy out. I was morbidly shy, no good at sports, mocked for reading the encyclopedia and the dictionary. Never once got in trouble. Never once. When Grandma got sick and Mom had to spend her time taking care of her, I took over. Cooked the meals, did the dishes, did the laundry, everything. Fourteen years old and I'm running the place. I should have been out setting fires or blowing up mailboxes, but to be honest, the one time I went with my friend Charles Holiday down to Mad River and we put firecrackers in frogs, it made me sick to my stomach. It still makes me sick to my stomach.

If I gave Guy the money he'd blow it, and I'd never see it again, but so what? I don't need it. I tell myself I might need it someday but the odds of that are easily calculable as nearly nil. Even if we decide to have children, my salary here plus frugal living plus careful investment equals never have to worry about money. And I have tenure, which is ridiculous, to give me tenure. I'm an indifferent teacher and a middling scholar. I will never achieve the kind of success worth dreaming about. Just to stay on top in a general way of developments in quantum chromodynamics is a full-time job, and everyone by now has a specialty that's more or less a specialization of a specialization of a specialty, and I don't have the kind of decisive temperament that allows me to put all my eggs in, for instance, asymptotic freedom, or quark confinement, because for whatever reason—and this is a sad thing for a quantum chromodynamicist to admit—my brain is too earthbound, too attached to the evidence of its senses for me to really engage with the flightier aspects of pure theory. I don't mean to say I don't understand/appreciate

$$\mathcal{L}_{\text{QCD}} = \bar{q}\left(i\gamma^{\mu}D_{\mu} - m\right)q - \frac{1}{4}G_{\mu\nu}^{a}G_{a}^{\mu\nu}$$

$$= \bar{q}\left(i\gamma^{\mu}(\partial_{\mu} + igT_{a}G_{\mu}^{a}) - m\right)q - \frac{1}{4}G_{\mu\nu}^{a}G_{a}^{\mu\nu}$$

$$= \bar{q}\left(i\gamma^{\mu}\partial_{\mu} - m\right)q - g\left(\bar{q}\gamma^{\mu}T_{a}q\right)G_{\mu}^{a} - \frac{1}{4}G_{\mu\nu}^{a}G_{a}^{\mu\nu}$$

$$= \bar{q}i\gamma^{\mu}\partial_{\mu}q - \bar{q}mq - g\bar{q}\gamma^{\mu}T_{a}qG_{\mu}^{a} - \frac{1}{4}G_{\mu\nu}^{a}G_{a}^{\mu\nu}$$

but I believe these things only halfheartedly, the way I believe in love, for instance, or the theory of evolution. Say you come up with the Theory of Everything, say you're that guy, the one who solves for all time the riddle to end all riddles. Would that make you happy? It would, I suspect, make me immensely, unfixably sad.

Used to be when I felt this way I would think about Constance, my wife, my so-called beloved. To whose wisdom I should always defer, because she is so much smarter than I am. At the end of the day, or really at any point during the day, or even at night, she tells me not to give Guy the money, Guy doesn't get the money. But she didn't tell me not to give Guy the money. I didn't even ask her. I've stopped asking her anything important. When did that happen?

The phone on Marcus's desk rang. He didn't seem to notice for several moments, then suddenly sprang forward as if the phone were a kind of alarm.

-Hello? Wait . . . slow down, Mom. You're not making any sense. What's wrong? Dad? What? Where did they take him?

Marcus checked his watch.

-I'll get the next plane to Dayton. Don't worry, I'm sure he'll be fine. I'm sure everything will be just fine.

5. WHAT GUY NEEDED, AND WHY: IN WHICH THE NOT ENTIRELY OMNISCIENT NARRATOR EXPLAINS THE KOREAN CHECK-CASHING FIASCO AND ITS INCITING INCIDENT, ABOUT TWO WEEKS BEFORE THE ACTUAL FIASCO. FOR THOSE INTERESTED, GUY IS SITTING ON THE COUCH IN HIS APARTMENT, WHICH THE READER WILL NEVER SEE AGAIN AND SO WE WILL NOT BOTHER TO DESCRIBE IT.

What Guy needed, above all, was the same thing everybody needs, all the time. He needed money. Not just knocking-around money, mind. He needed a substantial sum—fifty thousand dollars—and quickly, which is never an easy thing to come by, especially when your only really well-developed skill is talking down to people. That's why Guy needed Billy, who had a complementary skill of talking up at people.

Through a combination of happenstance and blind luck, which by the way are not the same thing, Guy had stumbled across a potentially useful technological invention, which to Guy meant lucrative, which by the way may or may not be the same thing, and he had tried, without success, to pitch the idea of this idea to a group of dead-eyed venture capitalists in Menlo Park a few weeks earlier. What he needed, they told him, was a working prototype. And to construct such a prototype, according to the naïve kid genius at Caltech who'd first clued him into the thing's existence, would cost fifty thousand dollars. It was beyond Guy's comprehension that no one would front him the fifty grand, but his friends in Los Angeles had all effectively laughed in his face, not at the idea of Guy's prototype, but the idea that any of them might have fifty thousand, or even five thousand dollars to lend him. Which is when he turned, much as he was loathe to do so, for a variety of complicated reasons, to his brother Marcus, who had brutally rejected him much the same way he had brutally beaten up Guy when he caught him cheating at *Monopoly* when they were teenagers, as if everybody doesn't always cheat at *Monopoly*, otherwise the game just goes on and on and on.

As time went by, and Guy's needs grew both more pressing and less obviously satisfiable, he and Billy got desperate enough to hatch Plan Charlie, which had not been preceded by Plans Alpha or Bravo, and in addition had nothing whatsoever to do with trafficking in cocaine.

Plan Charlie was in fact thus-branded because it depended for success on a guy named Charlie who worked at the check-cashing place on Washington and Pico in Koreatown. Charlie wasn't Charlie's real name, most likely, because he was Korean, but his name tag read *Charlie* and he answered to "Charlie" and when you paged him and he called you back he would say, "This is Charlie, you paged me?" All of which goes to show how far we've come, as a nation, when a man of Asian descent can call himself "Charlie" without a hint of self-awareness regarding the name's derogatory associations stemming from its use in Vietnam as slang for the enemy.

The plan was simple. The check-cashing place was particularly cash-rich on exactly two days per month, the first and the fifteenth, when most people got paid, or got their

Social Security checks. The money came in by armored car before eight a.m., usually even earlier, by six or seven, so that there'd be time to count and sort everything before the store opened at nine.

It's easy to rob a check-cashing place. It's far more difficult to do so successfully, meaning not just to "get away with it," because any fool can get away with any fool thing, but to make it worth your while, to come away with more than just a couple of bags full of twenties amounting to less than ten grand: that's virtually impossible, in fact, owing to a system most check-cashing places have devised to limit their inevitable losses from inevitable robberies. According to this system, no teller has more than $12,000 at any one time in his or her own personal drawer, which can be accessed only with his or her personal code, which even the store manager doesn't know. In order to spring all the drawers in the event of some unforeseeable emergency, you have to get a code from the head office, and that code is changed daily, guarded by a pit of fire and a sentient seven-headed cobra at the top of Mount Olympus, or something. At the end of the day, each teller enters his or her own personal code into his or her own personal drawer, and withdraws what's left after a day of usurious transactions. The accounts are then meticulously reconciled, the remaining money locked away in an earthquake-proof safe with an algorithmically absurd combination.

There was only one flaw in the system, and that flaw, as with all flaws in all systems, was human. At a certain vulnerable point in every process, in every system, an element of trust is required. That element of trust is the point of exploitation. In the case of Plan Charlie, that point of exploitation was Charlie.

Charlie was the assistant store manager, and as such the final check between cash distribution from the vault or armored car and the tellers' window drawers. It would be an easy matter for him to skim four thousand from each of the twenty-five prepared drawers (tellers worked in shifts, so second-shift drawers were prepared in advance) and put that money in a specially prepared drawer that he would tend himself, at Window 3, at exactly nine a.m. on the morning of the date chosen for the heist.

Guy and Billy would then roll in, disguised with ski masks and New York Jets football jerseys (this was Billy's contribution to the plan), brandish a fake gun in Charlie's face, and make off with what everyone who worked at the store would assume was $12,000, but would in fact be $100,000, which would then be split fifty to Guy, thirty to Charlie, fifteen to Billy, who after all wasn't really doing much, and five to the getaway driver. Charlie would slip out the back door before anyone noticed he was gone, and meet up with the others at a predetermined spot out in the desert.

Because the check-cashing place carried a considerable amount of insurance, all parties concerned considered this an essentially victimless crime, neglecting to reflect that a) they themselves might be the victims, or b) the pensioner who lived day-to-day on his Social Security check might now have to wait a few extra days, and what if he didn't have any food at all in his house, or what if he had to pay his rent and they kicked him out on the street and he died? He would certainly count as a victim.

6. SUBSENSORY ADVERTISING (ENABLED BY PANDEMONIUM'S REVOLUTIONARY TECHNOLOGY)—SLIDE 23 OF A 47-SLIDE POWERPOINT PRESENTATION ASSEMBLED BY GUY FOR THE BENEFIT OF POTENTIAL INVESTORS, A PRESENTATION, AS HAS BEEN NOTED, THAT FAILED MISERABLY IN THE ABSENCE OF A BETA-TESTED PROTOTYPE

The white brilliance of words. He said to Certainly don't mean strong are king of that was alongside, the winter. It have been described, as the original intention, veins. You came and evil time, and the Empire will be bored by the stalemate have decided to our customs, in the other titles was met that Trantor. But what ways of an individual in warm air and, darn little too, deep: in mind the ship, is only them. Your opinion Gaal flushed and your job (him and to allow collect his eyelids were)? What is not suffered a week or any grumbling, the; shadows. Then at that you win the coming to see it: wouldn't talk. That tin's my terms of other time. I have and He was the huge, glossy finish was. What would stand the Galactic spirit to rise but a closed for instance, the intruder Commission of a conglomerate be understandable! Now; after each depends in dry chuckle. Yes. Then: the appreciation, which is may seem got to be used in events of which places with I a few stars aimed his answer. If Fara bestirred himself, on Cygni all I could was only councilman and turned to receive, can be an Outright treason. That I'm not easily but so long; ago. I understand me why shouldn't we haven't got to the; cleverest politician on the time and Mallow out, toward that wouldn't I do: you doing? You Hahdin, that the wilds of you a question of single frosted trading here, said querulously. But by divine right. It could pick his was large as the word went: on that a bit god I have Anacreon exactly as all the head; there is to ask; for who work for it and who can't get out a condemned man: that, must do you know Surely, were heading; when I know me Where you're on on that was Gorov's voice, as the Grand Master's eyelids dropped, to all about that has based on Mallow looked up the Foundation when it has that it with the desk. I shall have will be one of in itself were all, the Emperor wars with it worked with. But at all, the whole trial was a life has the matter of the rim there replied never been in a hundred percent was one did you? Come from the gold of selling and disaffection within the greatest end; we might be to accept exile. Twer bitterly; or else: you send their religion half the admiral had to inflexible fact, that is important project is over the other, things more quickly: from his lower lip in the it would you see that. Now on the reports; and walked have placed the viceroy's Imperium: we can adjust the true, Ponyets (added, Sutt blinked and then the figures: in itself that humanity for good psychology is at all). The poor administrators: unloading platform. With an interesting he might pass The debarkation there in: two SELDON, had in order and it may be, carried, almost as and the cigar! Mob in the gallery caught in and said, the Five hundred percent of being stopped. Mission, to get that one kingdom outside the whole damned afraid the Galaxy. I have told him, with city in Terminus, traders need with a realm of the overall history of us so interested in your supply; bear carry on on the Empire and all!

7. THE TIME GUY'S FATHER VISITED GUY IN LOS ANGELES AND TOOK HIM OUT TO DINNER AT THE PALM, ABOUT TWO MONTHS BEFORE THE KOREAN CHECK-CASHING FIASCO

You don't eat meat? She doesn't eat meat?

–A lot of people don't eat meat, Dad.

–Not where I come from.

–You realize you don't actually come from the '50s. You just grew up then, said Guy.

–Dayton, Ohio. Pine Club. Best goddamn restaurant in the free world.

–That's actually true, more or less, but only if you eat meat.

–Lines out the door on the coldest day of the year. Can't make a reservation. They don't take 'em. One time, the President of the United States . . .

–Heard this story only about half a million times, Dad.

–Yeah, well, Violet hasn't. Have you, Violet?

–Nuh-uh.

–President comes driving up, Secret Service guys get out, go in, manager says, Sorry, we don't take reservations, President has to wait in line like everyone else. And he does. Two fucking hours. Of course, he waited out in his limo, but you get the point. If the Pine Club is worth two hours of the President of the United States' time, must be pretty damn good.

-Wow.

-You bet your skinny vegetarian ass, wow.

-Dad!

-I was joking. She knows I was joking. You didn't mind, did you, honey?

-Of course not. Guy, please punch your father in the face to defend my ass's honor.

-Now that's what I'm talking about! I like this one.

-Good to know, Dad. Your endorsement means so little to me.

-Respect for your elders. I tried to teach him, Violet, I really did. Never took.

-In fairness, you never really tried to teach me. Anything.

-If that's how you want to remember it, I can't stop you.

-And respect is something earned, not granted automatically.

-You know how I got where I am, said Robert, turning back to Violet. -Count every penny. Every goddamn one. Ask Guy. He remembers.

Guy remembered. Sifting bags of filthy coins into the automatic counter, reading off the total to his mother, who scrupulously kept the books. You could never get that smell off your hands, your skin, out of your hair. The whole house aromatic with copper, nickel, and dirt—every pore in the wood, every crack in the linoleum. Human dirt passed from coin to coin, coins pressed into sweaty palms, coins jangling in lint-lined pockets, coins dug out from between couch cushions, swept from under the bed, picked from the gutter. Guy had developed an aversion early on to handling currency in any form other than paper, which held terrors of its own, so even then with some distaste.

-What do you mean, Mr. Forget? asked Violet inevitably.

-I had most of the juke box concession for the entire Midwest region, said Robert. His ruddy face and cratered nose betrayed him as a longtime heavy drinker, a trait Guy had inherited, along with the ability to hold his liquor.

You don't grow up in an environment like that without permanent scars. Foremost among these an embossed stamp of embarrassment on your cheek that only you can see, but you see it all the time, whether looking in the mirror or in the mind's eye. This stamp, or emblem, this scarlet letter, B for Briar, is a thing you will go to great lengths to conceal or overcompensate to erase—unless or until it works to your advantage, which you'd be surprised how often that can happen in a place like Los Angeles, where anything out of the ordinary can work to your advantage.

8. PROMPTED BY HIS FATHER'S CONVERSATION, GUY HAS A MENTAL FLASHBACK TO HIS CHILDHOOD IN DAYTON, OHIO, WHILE SITTING IN THE RESTAURANT PRETENDING TO LISTEN

Pulling into the parking space in front of the bank in his father's Cutlass, Guy Forget had the impression of berthing a small schooner. The rump of the car sagged almost to the ground under the weight of its trunk's cargo; as a result the car's nose lifted at a haughty angle, and imprecisely responded to the shift of its wheels, as if resenting an imposition it had borne without comment for too long. Guy parked the heavy Oldsmobile with practiced care, and withdrew from the backseat a hand truck which he dragged behind him with one hand, groping with the other for the keys he had stupidly shoved in his jeans pocket before unlocking the trunk.

Heat. The keynote of the new day resounded dully in Guy's brain as he fumbled with the car keys. Though much of Third Street still lay swathed in blue shadow, long fingers of sunlight groped the dingy crevices between the bank and the adjacent drugstore, pooling on the latter's green-and-white-striped awning, leaving the sullen windows beneath to swelter darkly. The sun-swollen leaves of a young sycamore, trapped in a square of dirt in front of the bank, spackled the cracks in the sparsely peopled sidewalk with a paste of piebald shade. The air was moist and heavy. A gang of cicadas sawed the heavy, moist air.

Bending to extract the first of a dozen or so hefty canvas bags filled with rolls of variously denominated coins from his trunk, Guy felt a rivulet of sweat snake from one armpit down toward his waist. His white T-shirt stuck in wet patches to his skin. He lifted the bag with two hands and plopped it on the hand truck, then another, and another, shifting and stacking them expertly so that in the end all fit. Guy was proud of his prowess at stacking the bags of coins. Saved time too—one trip instead of two. And safer. Wouldn't have to leave any sitting in the trunk while he went into the bank.

He exhaled gratefully as he entered the musty cool of the old bank, pushing his hand truck through the darkly tinted glass doors. An elderly customer with a red jowly face, wearing a faded straw hat, stood before one of the two tellers, staring bemusedly at his passbook. Guy wheeled across the floor to the unoccupied teller.

It would be so easy, thought young Guy, to swivel the hand truck back out the door, repile the bags in the trunk, and jet out of town. Who would even miss me? Dad would miss the money before he missed me, but he'd get over it. Can't be more than ten thousand bucks in here. That's peanuts to him, but it's a year of independence for me. Marcus would be glad to be rid of me, he considered, there can be little doubt about that. And Mom . . . it's always difficult to know what's going on in Mom's head at any given time. Probably Mom's where I learned to hide my true feelings. In any case, Mom would be the key to the whole plan. Because eventually I'd run out of money, and I'd have to come crawling back home, the prodigal son in his tattered rags, and while Dad wouldn't want to take me back, and Marcus would act like I wasn't there, I could probably count on Mom at least to feed and clothe and bathe me. I don't know why I thought bathe. I didn't mean physically bathe. Obviously. I meant allow me to bathe. Because I assume that, on the run as I would be, I wouldn't have much time to bathe.

Which, on second thought, is sufficient deterrent to prevent me from swiveling the hand truck and following my plan. Someday, though, thought Guy. Someday I will follow through. I just don't know with what, exactly.

9. GUY AND BILLY DISCUSS PANDEMONIUM, SITTING IN BILLY'S APARTMENT, FOUR DAYS BEFORE THE KOREAN CHECK-CASHING FIASCO

The concept is good. We're agreed that the concept is good.

-If you say it's good, then obviously I trust you.

-I'm happy to hear that, but I'd be more happy if you understood what I'm trying to say. Who would not be attracted to this idea? I mean from a business standpoint. Advertising that's not advertising. Data collection that's invisible and untraceable.

-I am totally on board with this concept and I get your vision, but in the pure consumery sense this is not my thing.

-What is that? The pure consumery sense.

-What do you mean "what is that?" It is what it says it is.

-But you've invented a word. Which in itself would not be so bad, people invent words all the time, out of necessity, when there's not an exact word available, but in your case you've invented a word that doesn't need to exist.

You've invented a word out of sheer laziness. Your brain for whatever reason couldn't form the words "as a consumer," because—and here I'm just spit-balling—you were trying to make yourself sound more complex than you are.

-I *am* more complex than I am.

-I'm not sure you even listen to the things that come out of your mouth.

-I've been told I'm a good listener.

-You are. You're a very good listener. You just should never talk.

-I could really go for a cheeseburger.

-For breakfast?

-You've never had a cheeseburger for breakfast? It's good.

-I'll take your word on that one.

-Thanks, Guy. Means a lot to me.

10. GUY PREPARES TO MEET HIS BROTHER MARCUS TWO WEEKS BEFORE THE KOREAN CHECK-CASHING FIASCO

The concierge at the Chateau nodded his usual greeting, into which Guy read headlines of condescension followed by lengthy articles unmasking the sham of his existence. Pulitzer stuff, really well-researched, thorough, irrefutable.

He continued walking through the lobby, sat at his usual table, and ordered a large pot of coffee, which he took strong and black. Hungover celebrities and their antic publicists, studio executives trading industry gossip, and the odd fraud or tourist. In Guy's eyes, the tourist was lower than a fraud. The tourist, he considered, was someone who skimmed like a water spider on the surface of life. Even a fraud gets wet.

Guy had two hours before his brother arrived. He'd offered to pick him up at the airport, but Marcus had insisted on taking a cab, which was typical of the subtle ways in which Marcus underlined his aversion to Guy's company—half an hour less he'd have to spend trying to think up conversational topics that wouldn't offend his younger brother's sense of self—in Guy's mind.

Two hours, then, to work out the way, exactly, he would pretend to try to convince Marcus to lend him fifty thousand dollars to product-develop and implement a closed beta version of Pandemonium, the successful completion of which would help make Guy not just obscenely wealthy, but a player, a man with clout, powerful enough to park without fear in any other man's reserved spot anywhere in town.

Not that he expected Marcus to actually lend him the money. Through the lens Guy often used to view the future (cracked and varicolored, if you must know), he could see Marcus nodding sagely as Guy explained the super-advanced technology that he was "borrowing" from some dweeb at Caltech. In essence, this technology would enable companies to slip subsensory ads onto any kind of website, unnoticed by the unwitting net-surfer but nevertheless effective. Probably.

It's true that Guy himself did not fully understand the technology, but he knew Marcus would, because Marcus was a physicist and thus by definition able to understand anything that inhabited the physical world. Even the virtual physical world. Something in the sub-sub-code of the site—the Caltech guy had explained that it was in fact a reverse kind of HTML, he was inspired by reading about this French street slang called *verlan,* where the kids basically just reversed words so that grown-ups couldn't understand, but it had evolved into an entire language, almost, so in fact you could call this code LMTH, because it functioned the same way, and was similarly unintelligible to even the hippest web programmers, which was about where Guy stopped listening, because the idea of a hip web programmer was too much, almost, to take.

No one would be turned off by garish Flash-based ads or annoyingly obvious product placement or banner advertising or hyperlinks to Amazon.com or anything at all, and no pop-up blockers or anti-spyware or software of any sort could filter out the subsensory ads. A site using this technology would be self-supporting after week one and profitable by the end of the first month. Because imagine, advertisers: you're pushing your products in an effective yet totally discrete way, and however you measure results, whether by page counts or click-throughs or actual sales, you *will see* results, and soon, and because you signed a nondisclosure agreement as part of the contract, you can't talk about the subsensory ad placement technology, which means no one else can copy it for probably about six months, and six months in Internet time is forever, certainly long enough to establish this new technology, code-named Pandemonium, as the forerunner, forefather-mother, motherfucking four-eyed godfather of what will eventually be seen as a Rubicon moment in webby history, which will probably require Jobs-Gates level canonization of the man behind the curtain, who is me, Guy Forget, the inventor of Web 3.0, the blood-drenched edge of the Internet.

Marcus would then take a long sip from the glass of whiskey and soda that he had ordered from the solicitous Chateau waiter, and shake his head sagely, saying something like, "Sorry, Guy, I just don't see it."

But the point, for Guy, was never about the money, as he well knew, and as Marcus well knew as well. Guy would find a way to get the money, with or without Marcus. Guy's victory was that he had managed to get Marcus to divert precious time from his precious scientific conference on paper-clip theory or whatever, simply to force him to say no to his face, so that he might later derive years of unsportsmanlike pleasure from *having been right*. Not that he wouldn't share the wealth, regardless: au contraire, for Guy that would be the sweetest revenge, doling out money freely to family and friends, the anti-Marcus, as foolish and fancy-free as his older brother was cautious and tight-fisted.

Should Marcus unexpectedly agree to loan Guy the money, all the better, because then Guy wouldn't have to go through with Plan Charlie, which after all, despite its incredibly low risk of failure, was not entirely foolproof.

11. THE VILLAIN SVEN TRANSVOORT, STILL IN HIS UNDISCLOSED LOCATION, TALKS ABOUT GUY'S BACKGROUND, AND MAKES BROAD, MOSTLY NONSENSICAL GENERALIZATIONS ABOUT CULTURE

Guy Forget claimed to have been born in Dayton, Ohio, a place so anonymous I believe it may not actually exist; it wouldn't surprise me one bit if Guy had simply made up the name of his hometown. Whether or not that's true, Guy Forget was certainly American, in fact a little too American in some ways, because since he was young, Guy dreamed of getting rich quick, which I believe to be the heart of the American dream. For Americans who are born into the condition, the phrase "get rich quick" means exactly what it says: that they will suddenly and without much effort come into enough money to live without care in a luxurious manner. They can buy whatever car and in whatever quantity suits them. They can buy not only a very nice house but several of these, not less than two and not more than five, one for each of the varied topographies offered by our great country: a beach house, a house in the country, a ski chalet, an apartment in Manhattan, and a Primary Residence in the city or town where their ostentatious wealth will most impress those who knew them when they didn't have any money.

For Americans who come here from other countries, particularly from Latin America, by which I mean any country south of the United States' porous border, "get rich quick" is a somewhat easier goal, as it means simply taking the most menial job on offer, which has the effect of immediately doubling or tripling the most money they've ever made in their lives, enabling them to immediately raise their standard of living, however humble, to new heights, and even allowing them to save enough money to send back home to less fortunate family members, in order that one day they, too, might be able to join them and share the dream.

Guy Forget came from the former category, and though he was not uneducated, like many of his type he spent a lot of time using that education and whatever native intelligence he possessed trying to figure out ways to avoid work of any kind, which though he was not born to the leisure class he nevertheless regarded as beneath his dignity.

I don't know when Guy arrived in Los Angeles, but I'm certain he wasn't born here. He had too much nervous energy, too much ambition, and far too much self-awareness to have grown up in a place where even those transplants who've lived here long enough assume the lazy, spaced-out air of oxygen-deprived mice who no longer recognize themselves, or their surroundings, or their purpose in life, and are not in any way bothered by this loss. Guy dodged and weaved among the inhabitants of Los Angeles impatiently, shaking his head in wonder at the wasted time on open, unembarrassed display, furious anytime he had to slow down or wait for anyone or anything, which was often and a lot. One of the main features of life in Los Angeles is slowing down and waiting. This applies not just where you'd imagine, as for instance in traffic, but in almost every aspect of daily life: in line at the coffee shop, in the aisles of the grocery store, at the gas station, in restaurants, at the movies, in a bar, at the mall, in parking lots and garages, and, most especially—and this was the thing Guy found most galling—in bed.

Guy was still young, and good-looking, though not, granted, "good-looking" in the way that many young men are good-looking in Los Angeles, but most of these are obsessive about their good looks, which is the only really self-aware or more accurately self-conscious aspect of the general population in Los Angeles. The majority of these "good-looking" men are either a) actors or b) homosexuals or c) both, so in the end Guy's less-than-perfect kind of looks (six feet tall, one hundred and sixty-five pounds, brown hair, narrow hazel eyes set back in a long oval face, thin, spidery fingers, thick lips) were sufficient, when combined with his disarming manner and insincerely insouciant approach, to provide him with more than his fair share of short-term bedmates. These were almost always procured in bars sometime between the hours of midnight and two a.m., which is closing time in Los Angeles, and the hour of decision in Guyville. Which is not to say that the decision was always or even ever in Guy's hands, so to speak, nor that the decision, or verdict, if you will, was always favorable.

The reader cannot imagine the distaste with which I share these personal details about the object of my abject hatred, learned bit by bit as I nursed my animosity. I present these details in the spirit of entomology: so that you can

see exactly what kind of bug I was prepared to extermi-
nate, and to help understand why.

12. THE NATURE OF BILLY'S DAY JOB REVEALED, AT BILLY'S APARTMENT, FOUR DAYS BEFORE THE KOREAN CHECK-CASHING FIASCO

Guy?
-Yeah.
-I gotta head out. Time to walk the dogs.
-Yeah.
-It's not like I want to walk the dogs. I need the money.
-That's fine. The issue is, you don't walk the dogs. You tie them to the bumper of your car and drive very slowly.
-The dogs are walking. I don't see the problem.
-People hire dog-walkers not just so that their dogs get exercise. It's an important part of their socialization. They need to interact with other dogs, and with humans. Not to mention the purely excretory function of the walk.
-Hell, they piss and shit all over the place. I have to hose down my bumper every time.
-Thanks for that.
-What?
-That mental image. It goes well with breakfast.
-You don't eat breakfast.

-Not now I don't.

-Sorry.

-No need to apologize. I don't eat breakfast.

-That's what I just . . .

-Here's the thing, Billy: in the future, the not-very-distant future, I believe that the literate rabble, meaning those who regularly read serious books, are going to want shorter and shorter sentences, paragraphs, and pages. No more than a few pithy lines per page. That's the direction we're headed. White space, my friend. The future belongs to white space.

-You mean like the phone book?

-Exactly not. We've been conditioned by our gigantic computer monitors and even bigger TV screens to acres and acres of canvas, much of which is admittedly cluttered with irrelevancies, but that's not the audience for whom I'm mixing my metaphors. Especially in a time of recession, or depression, or whatever catastrophe lies in wait around the corner, like a kitten or a tiger, depending on your view of the relative stature of the world—especially now, minimalism will rule the day. In every sense, in every part of everyone's life. We're all going to become minimalists.

-You really shouldn't drink so much coffee, said Billy.

-Coffee is the original smart drug. I believe it actually makes me smarter. For instance: I've totally flipped my position on your dog-walking. My caffeine-fueled brain squall has traced a lemniscate around my original repulsion. You, my friend, are a trendsetter. Your dog-walking method is revolutionary in its simplicity. Is it cruel? Is it lazy? Is it not entirely sane? Doesn't matter. It cuts corners, and that's what we do, Billy. That's what Americans do. We cut corners. You don't achieve minimalism without sacrifice, and if at all possible that sacrifice should be shouldered by other people, or in this case dogs. I salute you, sir! You are a true child of Pandemonium, which even though it doesn't yet exist except in theory—and I admit it's possible may never actually exist—is the inevitable result, the culmination, of our ineluctable shift from being to nothingness.

Billy stood for a moment, nonplussed, unsure whether Guy was making fun of him.

-Time to walk the dogs, he said after a few moments.

-Yes it is! replied Guy. -Go forth and subtract!

13. GUY PITCHES THE IDEA OF PANDEMONIUM TO MARCUS IN THE LOBBY OF THE CHATEAU MARMONT, TWO WEEKS BEFORE THE KOREAN CHECK-CASHING FIASCO

Marcus took a long sip from his whiskey and soda.
-Still not getting it, Guy. Sorry.

-It's also a sophisticated data mining system. Advertisers will pay for page views, right, but they'll pay even more for detailed demographic info that enables them to target consumers with such specificity that everyone will think that the company is speaking to them.

-What makes you think people want companies to speak to them?

-They don't. But they'd rather see stuff they're actually interested in—like that machine that holds all your books and newspapers and magazines and displays them just like a paperback book . . .

-I've seen those. Not interested.

-Really? I want one. And Christmas is coming. Hint. Listen, Marcus, what we have in this country is an intel gap, and it's nothing to do with terrorists. The pace at which technology is changing is too fast for companies to keep tabs on trends in their own businesses. Think of Pandemonium as an enormously customizable Kindle. You want a snapshot of what kind of shoes twenty-three-year-old Asian women who work for one of the Big 12 accounting firms are buying? Or will be buying six months from now? Pandemonium can give you that. So in this sense, yes, Marcus, it's B2B, but it's also potentially P2P because a site running Pandemonium could in theory offer users the ability to file-swap freely with both anonymity and legality. Because the evil record company monoliths that will be secretly advertising on the site will be able to direct the consumer's file-sharing preferences, and further, to collect highly specific personal data, or metadata, I'm not really sure what metadata is but I think it sounds better, don't you? And buried deep down at the bottom of an unreadable EULA will be language giving them the right to do whatever they want with that information. With any information that they gather in any way at any time. But here's the thing: no one will worry, no one will complain, because they won't be getting spammed, they won't be getting *If you liked that, you'll like this* recommendations when they visit the site, they won't be getting *Welcome back, User Name!* They'll be getting targeted advertising, but they won't even know it. We offer the fiction of what everyone always thought the Internet should be—open source, free, unclogged, unmarketed, anonymous, collective: it's everything the twittering classes want but don't know they want.

–How do you know it works?

–Irrelevant. Let me put it to you this way: there's nothing viral about these new forms of communication, of social interaction, Marcus. The kids don't need *better*, they need or at least want *new*. A virus mutates and adapts to survive, but most of these virtual mutations will not survive. Which is not Darwinian, because nobody really understands that you can't apply the evolution of species to the evolution of ideas. Apples and pomegranates. Did you know there's a networking site called Spacebook? It's just for potheads. And Tracebook. That's for stalkers. These networks will target groups more and more specific until everyone has his own network to which he alone belongs. It's inevitable.

-I'm not sure . . .

-Thus, therefore, ergo, the chief virtue of Pandemonium—well, okay, one of its chief virtues—lies in its adaptability. Like any good parasite, we can shift from delivery service—IM, Skype, Twitter, Fluxus, Squeak, Trap Soul Door—to delivery service, ping-ponging all over the 3G spectrum. Undetectable as love, we go where you go. We follow the action. And in so doing, we *become* the action.

-Exactly how much coke did you do before meeting me?

-This is my brain not on drugs. Scary, right?

Marcus looked at Guy over the rim of his upraised glass. -What a waste of a mind.

-You stole that line from Dad.

-He said that?

-Right, because it doesn't sound like anything he would say.

-Great minds . . .

-. . . come to the same facile and entirely flawed conclusions. Is, I believe, the phrase you're groping for.

Marcus sighed, shook his head. -I say again: how do you know it works?

-How do you know anything works? I mean, there's

still people, and I'm on the fence about this one, who insist the moon landing was staged on a back lot here in Los Angeles, that there's no proof. The beauty of any new concept is that proof is in the eye of the beholder. Remember when that electric two-wheeled thingy was supposed to revolutionize urban transportation, solve all our congestion problems, get rid of pollution, etcetera?

–Yes. The Segway.

–Yeah, well, there were a lot of very smart people who bought into that idea in the secret prototype phase. Very smart and very rich people, I might add. And not a single one of them stopped to think, *Yes, okay, it works, but won't anyone on one of these things look incredibly gay?*

–How is that applicable to your project?

–It's like you're not even listening. You want another one? Guy signaled to a passing waitress.

Marcus nodded yes and tipped back his glass, the half-melted ice clacking against the rim.

–You're not going to give me the money, are you?

–No. In the first place, I don't even understand the name. Why Pandemonium? That's not a name that says "safe investment" to me.

–Wrong. I mean right, but wrong. The VCs I'll be talking to don't want safe. They're desperately afraid of missing out on the next big boat, and they don't care if it's the *Titanic*, because that was, let's face it, a historic boat, a boat people will always remember, even before the movie. In any case, the name's just a come-on. It doesn't mean anything specific. It just gives a sense to potential investors that something new is going to happen.

–Why would I pay simply for novelty?

–You wouldn't, Marcus. None of the Marcuses you've

ever been your whole life would ever pay for that. Just like you'd never pay for sex.

–You don't know that.

–Have you? Ever?

–Not yet. But just because something hasn't happened yet doesn't mean . . .

–Stop playing really-annoying-grad-student for one damn minute.

–I'm not . . .

–I know. I was making a point. Jesus, it's like you've never heard anyone but yourself talk.

–Sorry.

–There's a lot of people, an awful lot, who *have* paid for sex. Who do pay for it. Who will continue to pay for it. It's a multibillion-dollar business. Bigger than movies and music and every other form of entertainment on earth combined.

–I'm not sure that's true.

–It doesn't matter if it's true. We're not selling sex. I'm making an analogy. Our pitch is that Pandemonium is better than sex.

–Who's "us"?

–See this? This is an imaginary stick. You've just grabbed hold of one end of the imaginary stick. You know which end? The *wrong one*.

–What's the difference? It's imaginary.

–Everything is imaginary, Marcus. Everything that's worth anything. Pandemonium is worth more than you can imagine, precisely because it's imaginary.

–I'm confused.

–Confusion is sex.

–What?

-Nothing. Obscure rock music reference. Couldn't help myself.

-That's the trouble with you, Guy. You have no self-discipline.

-And the trouble with you, Marcus, is that you have nothing *but* self-discipline. There's no goal. No purpose. You keep at it and at it, you're dogged and determined and all those dreary adjectives, but toward what end?

-Now who sounds like a grad student?

-*Touché*, asshole. Last chance: you going to lend me the money or not?

-I'm leaning toward not.

-I'm leaning toward the floor. Buy me a drink.

-You have a drink.

-I mean *another* drink. Obviously. Cocksucker.

13A. MINUTES LATER, MARCUS GOES TO THE BATHROOM, JUST AT THE MOMENT HIS WIFE CONSTANCE, WHO ACCOMPANIED HIM TO LOS ANGELES FOR THE QUANTUM CHROMODYNAMICS CONFERENCE, WALKS INTO THE LOBBY OF THE CHATEAU MARMONT LOOKING FOR HER HUSBAND—AGAIN, ABOUT TWO WEEKS BEFORE THE KOREAN CHECK-CASHING FIASCO

Guy's heart sank at the sight of Constance. Constance's heart sank at the sight of Guy. He motioned for her to take a seat, which she did reluctantly.

-He'll be right back, said Guy. -Men's room.

-Okay. Good.

An awkward silence developed between Guy and Constance, a vacuum that somehow the ambient chatter of the rest of the lobby's guests could not fill.

-You doing all right? asked Guy, for lack of anything else to say.

-Why bother pretending, Guy?

-Okay. Fine. Look, Constance, I love my brother. I mean, I don't like him very much, and he doesn't like me, but that's cool, that's fine. By extension, I'm supposed to love you too. Or at least like you. You're family. I'm told family is important. I don't know why it's important, but that's what I hear. That's the word on the street.

-You live on a strange street, Guy.

-Is this really just about the teeth-brushing thing?

-I'd call that symptomatic of a deeper problem.

-Because I'm willing to do a lot to satisfy my familial responsibilities. I mean, not really, but I might consider certain changes if they were reasonable. But I'm not going to brush my fucking teeth just because my brother's wife thinks it's disgusting.

-I'm not crazy about your haircut either.

-This is the nub of our problem, Constance. I don't care what you think.

-I'm not sure you want to say *nub*.

-Yeah, whatever.

Silence once again descended like a grade-school play curtain between the two.

-What the fuck is he doing in there? said Guy after a while.

-Brushing his teeth, replied Constance, with a sarcastic smile.

14. THE NIGHT GUY MET VIOLET MCKNIGHT, FIVE MONTHS BEFORE THE KOREAN CHECK-CASHING FIASCO

The Smog Cutter doesn't look like much from the outside. It doesn't look like much from the inside either, but its grime is its charm, apparently. Grime and karaoke—which at the time Guy met Violet had not yet become the hipster cliché it has since become. In other words, although those who participated in the nightly karaoke sessions at the Smog Cutter did so largely in quotation marks, these quotation marks still had a certain fresh appeal, had not yet worn out their welcome in the smugly insular world of Los Angeles' bohemian class. It was therefore not unusual to find famous rock musicians, like the bald singer from R.E.M., and famous actors, like the thin blond girl from the *Charlie's Angels* remakes, rubbing elbows and too-sharp rib cages with ordinary Beck-a-likes in trucker hats with sideburns and horn-rimmed glasses.

The drinks were cheap, though watered down, and you had to wait forever for your turn at the microphone, which would usually get hijacked by one of the celebrities anyway. Guy found it incredibly annoying to get halfway through the first verse of Supertramp's "The Logical Song" only to be interrupted by an overeager and tone-deaf Rising Starlette wearing a gray satin slip dress that clung to her erect nipples like saran wrap. Who would then spill her rum and Coke on the sleeve of Guy's only good jacket, laughing at herself in an attempt to prove that she was capable of laughing at herself.

-Why did you go, then? asked Violet, several weeks later, in languid repose on her reposable futon.

-Same reason everybody goes. There was nothing else to do. Why were you there?

-Free drinks. The Chinese lady who runs the place likes me. I think she's a lesbian.

Guy nodded. -Free drinks is a really good excuse.

The night Guy met Violet, she was sitting at the bar in a white dress with a white feather boa around her neck, long before feather boas became either fashionable or ironically fashionable, and on Violet looked unaffectedly sexy. Her hair was dark brown, medium-length and tousled, with shiny turquoise clips placed at seeming random, and her lipstick was red and her fingernails were red and her toenails were red and her eyes—like the two small tattoos on the back of her neck and on her left shoulder, abstract curlicues—were green.

-It's my birthday, said Guy, pushing his way to the bar through the unruly crowd, into a space next to Violet, who looked him over and smiled mutely. It was, of course, not Guy's birthday, that was his standard opening line, and he had waited three drinks before summoning the courage to talk to Violet, who had attracted his attention on several earlier nights, and again tonight, the moment Guy pushed through the red plastic strips that hung just inside the front door, outside of which, in the gray Los Angeles night, the doorman knew Guy well enough not to ask to see his ID. The shiver of pleasure you get when a doorman recognizes you, when you have become a regular, when you are no longer entirely anonymous in a city that loves to deliver crushing reminders of your anonymity regularly, right to your face, was one of Guy's favorite small triumphs.

-Can I buy you a drink to celebrate my happy occasion? Guy continued, noticing that Violet had not stopped smiling or looking at him since he had spoken to her, and taking this as a sign of encouragement.

-What's your name? asked Violet.

-Guy.

-That's a funny name. Guy. What's your last name?

-Forget. My name is Guy Forget. It should be pronounced For-*zhay*, but no one ever does. Just like my first name should be pronounced *Ghee*, but no one ever does.

-Why not?

-I don't know. They just don't. When I was younger that used to bother me, but it doesn't now.

-My name's Violet.

-Like the flower?

-Yes. Which brings us to the limit of my interest in gardening. I hope you have something else to talk about.

-I've seen you in here before.

-I come here a lot. So do you.

-And yet we've never met. Until now.

-On your birthday.

-It's not really my birthday.

-I figured that out already, *Ghee*.

-How?

-Because you wouldn't waste your birthday talking to me, a stranger. You'd spend it with friends.

-If I had any.

-Everybody has friends.

-Not everybody.

-Some people even have too many friends.

-Agreed. How about that drink?

Violet shook her head. -I don't need another drink. I need a cigarette. You want to go have a cigarette with me?

-I don't smoke. But I'll watch you smoke.

-Okay.

Outside, the light had followed its usual progression from gray to dull orange, the color of night in Los Angeles, and Guy trailed Violet around the side of the building so as to be away from the bustle of Vermont Street. Violet pulled out a yellow pack of cigarettes from her small black purse, but before she could use the matches from the bar, Guy leaned in and kissed her.

-You kissed me, said Violet, touching her fingers to her lips.

-Sorry.

-We hardly know each other.

-That's true.

Violet snorted derisively. -Let's go to a different bar, she said.

-Okay. Are you driving?

-No. I came with a friend.

-I'll drive then. Do you need to tell anyone you're leaving?

-No. Do you?

-No.

-Can I drive your car?

-*Baby, you can* . . . actually, no. It's better if I drive. My car's kind of touchy.

-Me too. Violet tossed her unlit cigarette on the ground and dropped to her knees, fumbling at Guy's zipper.

-No, stop. Someone might see, protested Guy.

-That's the whole point, whispered Violet into Guy's ear as he pulled her to her feet. Her tongue darted quickly into the folds of his outer ear.

Guy pulled her close and tried to kiss her again. Violet turned her head away.

-Where are you parked? she asked.

It was approximately at that moment that Guy fell for Violet, fell hard, fell for good. It's not right to say "fell in love" because it's not clear that either Guy or Violet was capable of love as commonly understood, which would require a certain degree of selflessness, however slight, that may have been beyond the abilities or at least inclinations of both. But Guy was, whatever else, enormously enamored.

What Violet felt was more difficult to determine, because Violet hated showy emotions, but it was clear that she liked Guy, maybe liked him a lot, or so it seemed to Guy, who did not wish to examine or question further his luck.

Violet was the sort of girl who seemed to exist to inspire infatuation. She did this intuitively, without trying, by obscuring her true intent and radiating, at every moment, a kind of pure possibility—promise in human form—that could not and did not fail to attract both the best and the worst kind of man. She took all comers, without discriminating, without judging, for reasons that she preferred to keep to herself, and most of her lovers did not care to question. Because behind that façade of possibility lay a steel curtain of Do Not Enter. Not physically, of course, because that was the easy part, requiring only physical desire and a fear, if you can call it that, of being alone. But emotionally, Violet was remote to an extreme not usually seen in a human being. Almost not actually present, which for anyone interested in a sustainable or long-term relationship—and there were many, some of whom would have left their wives, children, houses, and vital organs behind for her sake—proved an immovable force.

Occasionally she formed attachments, however: men she liked more than usual, and whose companionship she enjoyed outside of the realm of sex, so long as they did not violate any of her inscrutable and often capricious rules. The first and foremost of which, as Guy would eventually learn, was, *Do not ask me any questions about myself.*

The Echo Lounge was only a two-minute drive from the Smog Cutter, but almost as soon as Guy pulled out of the parking lot, Violet reached for his crotch.

-What are you . . . he began, then trailed off as Violet shifted in her seat and bent over his lap.

-We don't really have time, he protested meekly. -We're practically there already.

-Just keep driving, said Violet, without looking up.

-Okay.

Guy kept driving, on unfamiliar streets, panicking whenever he pulled up at a stoplight, as if anyone in an adjacent car was interested in what was going on in his, or would be even if they knew. Los Angeles by its nature attracts only the most self-absorbed inhabitants from all corners of the globe—in other words, if it wasn't happening to them, personally, or at second best to a very famous person, then it wasn't happening at all. The process took all of ten minutes, after which Violet sat up in her seat, licked her lips, and smiled broadly.

    -Let's get a drink, she said.

    -Okay.

15. GUY AND BILLY DISCUSS PROCEDURE IN RE: PLAN CHARLIE SITTING IN THE PROBABLY STOLEN MINI COOPER IN THE PARKING LOT OF THE KOREAN CHECK-CASHING PLACE MERE MINUTES BEFORE THE ACTUAL FIASCO

A re we clear vis-à-vis procedure? asked Guy.
-I'm not even sure I know what that means.

-I mean, do you know what you're supposed to do?

-Yes.

-And you're okay with it?

-I'm not *not* okay.

-Billy.

-I suppose you could say I have a few moral qualms. Still.

-Still?

-We're stealing money that belongs to someone else.

-We're not stealing the money. We're reifying the money.

-No matter how many times you say that . . .

-Reification is a perfectly valid process, as long as its use is intentional. Money, as a thing-in-itself, does not exist. It's an extended metaphor for a complex system of commodity exchange. Thus, to think of money as "belonging" to someone or something is a pathetic fallacy, in the literal sense. It's our job, as self-appointed stewards of the language, to liberate money from its normative bonds. There is no quick-and-easy shortcut. I wish there were. We have to go in and actually do it. Hence Plan Charlie.

–I thought you just needed cash to fund the prototype for Pandemonium and your asshole brother wouldn't loan you any.

–There's that too. But he's not an asshole. It's not your place to judge. You don't judge a blind man for his lack of vision.

–Usually not. But what if he stabbed both of his eyes out with a fork?

–Why would you . . . why would you even *say* that?

–Wasn't there a Greek tragedy about a guy who clawed his eyes out with like his bare hands?

–Tell it to your therapist.

–He's the one who told me. Couldn't sleep for a week. That's a disturbing image to plant in a five-year-old's brain.

–It's almost time.

Billy opened the glove compartment, carefully removed an object in a filthy, oil-stained rag, carefully unwrapped the rag to reveal the glistening shaft of a handgun.

–You sure this is fake.

–Here's the thing, Billy. I've planned every aspect of this operation within an inch of our lives. Some would say I've overplanned, but I don't believe you can overplan, I don't believe you can be too prepared, it's just the way I operate. Do you think, can you imagine, in the vasty dim cobwebbed caverns of your brain, that I would neglect something as absolutely crucial as ensuring that you were equipped with a weapon that in no conceivable way could be used as a weapon, because to do otherwise would be to court certain death?

–So you just assumed.

–The man said it was fake. Like I'm gonna check?

Billy lifted the gun in his right hand, measured its heft in his palm.

–Kind of heavy for a fake.

–Look, just don't shoot anyone. Okay? I mean, in case. That way it's not an issue.

–It's not like I was planning on shooting anyone.

–Good.

16. SVEN TRANSVOORT AT THE SMOG CUTTER, THE SAME NIGHT GUY MET VIOLET, FIVE MONTHS BEFORE THE KOREAN CHECK-CASHING FIASCO

S he left, right through that door. Didn't even say anything to me, didn't look back. Clinging to that strange-looking fellow. All kissy-eyed and tulip-faced. Does she not know how much that hurts me? Does she not care? Violet McKnight, I love you. I get such joy out of looking after you. Buying you clothes, taking you out to lunch and dinner, lending you cash—as if I don't remember what it's like living from paycheck to paycheck. And the reluctance with which you ask—it breaks my heart. I have to practically drag the words from your mouth, which to be honest I would prefer to do with my tongue, but I agree, it's better to wait, because waiting heightens the anticipation, and sex only muddles the emotions. I will wait until you're ready.

Who could not respect the fact that, however much I plead and argue, she refuses to give up her job, despite that the long hours and the stress, which keeps her away from me intolerably long, and delivers her to me too tired to do anything but collapse on my bed? I happily cede you my bed, dear Violet. The couch is fine for me, because it's close to you, but not too close, not so close that we would fall prey to our natural instincts. I need only nearness, proximity, the aura of your umbra, and I understand and approve of your need for space. When I hear your hesitant knock at my door, late at night, if you knew with what febrile glee I leap from my seat at the dining room table, where I've been writing another of those letters you cherish so much, but that cost me so little effort, because they pour straight from the source of my longing for you onto the page, and open the door to see your hesitant smile—if you knew that, dear Violet, why would you walk out the door of the Smog Cutter, which is a ridiculous name for a bar, in the first place, and in the second place, karaoke?—with a complete stranger, who is first of all obviously gay, though he may not be aware of it, which I find to be a common condition in Los Angeles, without a word of explanation?

The answer is of course obvious: she's testing me. It's true that my jealousy does at times get the better of me, and that jealousy, as Violet once said, is an allergic reaction to the presence of ego. But there are only so many rum and Cokes a man can sit and drink by himself, listening to some god-awful blonde twig butcher Supertramp's sublime "The Logical Song," before he takes it upon himself to investigate your disappearance.

So I fail the test. *Mea maxima culpa*, darling. I am human after all, it turns out. A thorough search of the parking lot turns up nothing but the hurried rustling of two lovebirds I accidentally disturb *in flagrante*, but soon thereafter a car engine starts, noisily, and is that, could that possibly be your silhouette, Violet McKnight, in the passenger seat of some carbon-belching rust-bucket, driven by the same clearly gay stranger with whom you'd walked out the door half an hour before?

You'll forgive me for stating the obvious: I got in my Prius and I followed you. Which was not an easy thing to do, because you did not appear to be headed anywhere in particular, and in fact kept circling around the same few blocks in Silverlake, where there was not enough traffic for me to keep anything but a discreet distance. Until you stopped at a red light on Vermont, a two-lane road, at last. I cautiously pulled alongside, and at first I didn't see you, dearest. And then I did. And then I didn't. And then I did.

In that moment I became Sven Transvoort. In that moment I became a monster, a caricature, a vengeance-minded machine. In that moment I understood everything about Guy Forget, even though I didn't yet know his name. I understood his cheap appeal, his reckless ways, and the unavoidable fact that he must die. And that I must kill him.

My hatred of Guy Forget flowered in my heart like bougainvillea: fragrant, bright, beautiful, but poisonous as any viper's venom. Obviously, bougainvillea isn't poisonous, but the hatred in my heart—pure neurotoxin. An atomized drop of that hatred breathed in by Guy Forget from one hundred yards away would have killed him instantly. The only problem was, there's no way to extract the poison from my heart without slicing open my chest, and there are some things I am not yet prepared to do in the name of revenge. That's one of them.

I can't think of too many others, however. For instance: things that I am totally prepared to do in revenge w/r/t G.F. would include but are not limited to: setting him on fire, shooting him in the face, and dosing him with incredibly high levels of LSD and leading him blindfolded to the top of the Capitol Records building and then taking off the blindfold and telling him he can fly.

But why deal in theory when you can deal in praxis, is my current motto, so what I did instead was 1) convince Guy Forget that I had invented a form of subsensory Internet coding that cannot possibly exist in any of our eleven dimensions, and 2) help set up the Korean check-cashing debacle and then sabotaged it.

Following the fiasco, I followed the hapless duo, discretely, in a car completely unlike the one I told Guy I would be driving. I watched them stop, and get out, and have a heated argument, and I watched them roll down the hill, and then I got scared and went home.

Oh sure, there's a flaw in every plan, no matter how brilliant or at least inspired and well thought out. I did not foresee that Guy would leave Billy, climb back up the hill, get back in the car, and drive at unsafe speeds toward wherever he thought he could find me—I assume that's where he was going, though perhaps my ego here overrides my reason—and in so doing crash the car and more or less die, by which I mean suffer damage to his cerebral cortex that effectively ended his conscious existence. I am not responsible nor do I care much about other planes of consciousness on which Guy Forget may or may not be able to function. I am, however, directly or at least directly indirectly responsible for his current comatose state, and I'm pretty sure that makes me an attempted murderer, whether or not he lives for years and years with tubes sprouting from his body like a potato. If he dies, either naturally or via some kind of state-sanctioned euthanasia, I am a murderer. This thought does not trouble me.

The risks one takes in the name of love. The things one does. Crazy, right? Sort of even death-defying. And for something so definitively transient, that passes the moment—the actual moment—it becomes realized . . . Well, I don't need to tell you good people the foolish feeling that washes over you after you've done something reckless and embarrassing, in the clear light of day, when you've regained your senses.

I do not regret what I did. He had to pay. He had to pay for what he did: he stole my dear, darling Violet, the one human being on earth to whom I offered my unconditional love and support. Stole her as easy as St. Augustine picked the peaches off a tree that did not belong to him, and then wrote a whole book about how sorry he was. Stole her and did not even love her, or *possibly* did not love her, at least I imagine he did not, because creatures like Guy seem to me incapable of love.

Having said that, even considering Guy Forget separately from his transgressions, dispassionately, with an open mind, it took me less than five seconds to realize that he was the most evil person on the planet, deserving both of unfettered disgust and the full and undivided attention of my bloody-minded revenge.

17. THE TIME GUY AND BILLY GOT IN A FIGHT AND FELL DOWN A HILL, MERE MINUTES AFTER THE KOREAN CHECK-CASHING FIASCO

Look at me. I'm bleeding in like a million places.

–You got a few scratches.

–A few scratches? We just fell all the way down that fucking hill! Look up there. Look!

–I'm looking.

–That's a pretty long way.

–It's kind of impressive, actually.

–Did you roll all the way? I feel like I maybe flew through the air a little bit. Like maybe I hit a clump of roots or a bush and actually went flying for a few feet.

–I don't know. It happened really fast.

–But it seemed to take forever.

–Weird.

–Yeah. Anyway, sorry about that. I kind of provoked you into pushing me, I think.

–I shouldn't lose my temper so easily.

–Well, I know how to push your buttons. And I know that I know. And I shouldn't do it.

-In a perfect world.
-Which we can agree that this is not.
-Yes.

18. "OH, MARCUS, WHAT THE FUCK IS YOUR PROBLEM ANYWAY?" REMARKS THE NOT ENTIRELY OMNISCIENT NARRATOR AS MARCUS VISITS HIS RECENTLY DECEASED FATHER IN A HOSPITAL IN DAYTON, OHIO, VERY CLOSE TO THE ACTUAL TIME OF THE KOREAN CHECK-CASHING DEBACLE

He looks peaceful.

-Well, most dead people do, Mom.

-You're not the kindest person in the world, are you, Marcus?

-I'm my father's son.

-Also your mother's son.

-No, that's Guy. Guy's much nicer than me. He got all the nice genes from your side of the family.

-I didn't say nice. I said kind. There's a difference. You're a very nice person, Marcus. You're responsible, reliable, even-keeled. You almost never lose your temper or snap at people.

-I get it. Guy's not really a nice person in that sense. But he is kind.

-Yes. And I think your father understood that, somewhere deep down.

-What makes you say that?

-The money he left Guy.

He left Guy money? After all those years of refusing to loan him anything?

-Exactly. I think he always planned that after he . . . passed on, Guy would get the money he wanted, and then your father wouldn't have to watch him—potentially—fail at whatever it was he wanted the money for.

-His last thing was something to do with some kind of new web-based technology. I didn't exactly understand.

-For getting rid of spiders?

-The Internet kind of web, not the spider kind.

-The kind that requires a loan from his brother.

-He seemed really keen this time. Or desperate. I'm not sure there's a big difference.

-And you said no.

-Yes. I said no.

-Well, now you can tell him yes. If not for yourself, at least on your father's behalf.

-You want me to tell him?

-I think it's appropriate.

-What's appropriate would be for him to be here, now. What's appropriate would be for him to have acted, just once, like a member of this family, like we weren't simply people he called when he was in trouble or needed something.

-He's never been good about remembering birthdays. It's not one of his strong points.

-I'd like to know what are his strong points. Other than annoying the hell out of Constance . . .

-Who's not here . . .

-Mainly because she was afraid Guy would be here.

-So now you're saying you're glad Guy's not here, because if he had been here, and your wife too, that would have caused a problem.

–She hates Guy because Guy never brushes his teeth. I mean, not brushing occasionally, that's forgivable, but never? That's just gross. But it's not the point, Mom. He should be here. And maybe Constance had other reasons for not being here. We've been having some issues lately and I didn't want to drag her into some big emotional family drama.

–Money or children?

–Those aren't the only things couples fight about, Mom.

–Then it's sex.

–Oh God. Please stop.

–I'm right, though. Do you want me to talk to her?

–I think I'll call Guy. How much money is he getting?

–Fifty thousand. After taxes.

–He'll be thrilled. That's exactly what he was looking for.

–He's not picking up.

–He's probably busy.

–Yeah. Hey, it's me, listen, good news–bad news thing. Dad's dead, but he left you a bunch of money. Fifty grand, to be exact. I figured you'd want to know. About both things. You won't call me back, but if you want the money you'll have to call Mom at least. Bye.

–You really are not a kind person.

No, Mom, I'm not. But who would be right now? Given the circumstances.

–Maybe you're right.

19. GUY, DRIVING IN HIS STOLEN CAR AWAY FROM WHERE HE LEFT BILLY AT THE BOTTOM OF A HILL AFTER THE KOREAN CHECK-CASHING FIASCO, WRITES A SONG, AS YOU DO

The hills are on fire. Literally ablaze, thought Guy, driving north on Larkin Heights, and it's not the sunset, it couldn't be, because the hills are to the north and the sun sets in the west, and in any case it's only around two in the afternoon.

Wretched Catullus, stop playing the fool and consider lost what is lost. But what does this mean: lost? There is no loss, only an accretion of circumstance, a heap of learning, a frantic scramble to retain focus while the walls of the world crumble. The walls of the world are always crumbling, it's their natural state. Inviolable entropy demands constant flux. Change is a brick wall that looks exactly like no change, and the headache you get from one is the mirrored throb of the other. I would like to lodge a protest against the notion of progress as reflected in the debased journalism of the marketplace. I would like to stand athwart history and spit. I would like a place I could call my own. I would like to tell better jokes.

In his head, at that moment—which turned out to be among his very last moments—Guy wrote a song, called "The Last Lonely Man."

The Last Lonely Man
words & music by Guy Forget

Verse (DGC)
Out of the corner of my eye I watch you walk on water
I'm not afraid to say goodbye
This is the room I fit in
I sleep, but
Not always
I'm not afraid to say goodbye

Bridge (AmDm)
And nobody's ever here
And nobody's left to hear

Chorus (CGDG)
He stares at the moon and sun
He's in love with everyone
The last lonely man's heart breaking
The last lonely man's heart breaking

Verse (DGC)
Out of the corner of my eye I see the water rising
I'm not afraid to say goodbye
This is the room I fit in
I sleep, but
Not always
I'm not afraid to say goodbye

Bridge (AmDm)
He lives on a riverboat
That will not, cannot float

Chorus (CGDG)
And the tide is always out
And that is all she wrote
The last lonely man's heart breaking
The last lonely man's heart breaking

C Section (DBF)
I'm crashing down, I'm crashing down
I'm crashing down, I'm crashing down
Back to the ground where I belong

Chorus (CGDG)

Fade Out (DGC)
(Many years in the making
Now he's yours for the taking)

20. THE VILLAIN SVEN TRANSVOORT SLANDERS VIOLET MCKNIGHT IN AN ATTEMPT TO JUSTIFY HIS ACTIONS, SITTING IN AN UNDISCLOSED LOCATION SEVERAL WEEKS AFTER THE KOREAN CHECK-CASHING FIASCO

Violet had been brought up to think that nothing she did could in any way be held against her, because she was entitled to act however she thought fit. Her sense of entitlement derived partly from some innate personality quirk, possibly inbred, but was equally the fault of a world that granted to girls of a certain age and a certain bearing and a certain way of moving through the world—as if they were the still center of that moving orb—an almost limitless degree of slack. If you were young, and attractive, and self-centered, without a thought in your head that did not concern either your immediate physical desires or your immediate-future physical desires, then you were given the real world equivalent of an All Access pass, and treated by most of the world in the way that you saw yourself, which, without putting too fine a point on the matter, is to say you saw only yourself, with the possible exception of those people or things who could supply you with whatever it is you might want, in which cases the near-total eclipse of everyone else's personality by your own would lift, for a moment, allowing a mild, refracted light to pinhole the gloom of your presence, only to resume when your restless vision set your restless feet in motion.

The good news, for those left behind, wondering *What the hell just happened?* as Violet continued on her way, was that the eclipse would soon lift entirely, and daylight (or nightlight, as the case might be) would resume its natural or artificial course, leaving, as in the Middle Ages before such phenomena had been adequately explained by science, only a sense of unease and mild confusion, which too will pass, class.

You can understand and even—I admit this may be going the extra mile, but why not go the extra mile?—empathize with a girl like Violet, who has never *not* gotten her way in the smallest of life's transactions, for instance when she didn't have enough money to pay for a six-pack of beer at the gas station, but smiled sweetly at the attendant, who told her to just go ahead, what's money anyway but a commodious vicus of recirculation. We are to blame, you understand, in this and all other instances. We are the force that drives a movie star to steal beautiful clothes from an expensive store even though she could easily afford the clothes—because when everything is given to you, there is no pleasure in receiving, only taking. We are to blame when a rich young man drives over the curb at five in the morning on his way home from a nightclub and plows his armor-plated luxury vehicle through the dark windows of a souvenir store, scattering T-shirts and baseball caps and coffee mugs and little plastic replicas of the Statue of Liberty all over the linoleum floor. That's our fault too, because the rich young man has no one he can really trust, and I will tell you why: because he is rich and young. And society preys on the young and the rich, we turn them into objects of fascination, into playthings, we use them up and spit them out, usually into a plate glass window, leaving them with an inadvisably high blood-alcohol content—also our fault, both for inventing alcohol and effectively marketing its miraculous powers—and a month-long stay in a rehabilitation center, which does not come cheap, because the rehabilitation of rich people is a serious, time-consuming, and expensive procedure, not unlike the artificial insemination of cows (or horses).

The dark victories Violet won, whether effortless or not, were so small in scope, so lacking in imagination and foresight, that the only appropriate reaction, as far as I was concerned, was to shake my head in wonderment. Full disclosure: I never slept with her. Usually when a man tells you he's slept with a beautiful girl you accuse that man of bragging. There's really no other reason for telling. You're making a statement, in the same way that a hunter who brags about bagging a twelve-point buck is making a statement: I'm good, he's telling you, I'm a good hunter. Stands to reason that I'm saying something the opposite of that: I'm no good, Sven Transvoort is telling you, I'm an ineffective sexual predator.

As such, as an unspurned nonlover, I can claim perfect objectivity with respect to Violet's peccadilloes. Which I am nevertheless, in the manner of an overindulgent step-uncle, perhaps too easily ready to forgive and forget, or at least forgive.

I have no similar inclination toward Guy Forget. Guy used girls like Violet to get things he could not easily get himself, but held no special affection for them. I'm not sure

Guy held special affection for anyone, except maybe Billy, but that's no excuse. She may have been many things, she may have *fait des bêtises*, but *that is no excuse*.

My point being that had Guy loved Violet more, or had she loved him less, none of this would have happened. In the end, though, you could fairly say that he got *everything that was coming to him*.

Please don't get me wrong. Violet was no angel, and I am anything but gallant. I don't rescue fair maidens. I don't slay dragons. I carry out personal vendettas. That's my thing. And to answer your unasked question, Mr. Dead Lennon, I sleep just fine at night, thank you very much.

21. THE ONLY TIME GUY VISITED VIOLET'S APARTMENT, OR, MORE PROPERLY PUT, THE ONLY TIME HE WAS ALLOWED TO DO SO, FIVE DAYS BEFORE THE KOREAN CHECK-CASHING FIASCO

Guy followed Violet into the murk of her living room. A sputtering fire—charred newspapers and the splintered skeleton of a chair—was being prodded laconically with an iron poker by a gloomy short-haired fellow, to whom she did not bother to introduce Guy.

As his eyes adjusted to the light he made out a rickety table, a mossy, anemic easy chair, and a cushionless couch backed against the farthest, darkest wall. Something that may have been a bookcase, now barren and partly stripped for kindling, was propped unsteadily against the amphibrachic couch. On the table by the easy chair were perched a squat stoneware lamp embossed with a blue dragon breathing green fire, and a telephone painted in several fluorescent colors, obscuring the numbers.

Above the mantel hung a large painting, about the size of a refrigerator door tipped on its side, in color and composition resembling the telephone. On the mantel itself were arranged a foot-high plastic Tyrannosaurus rex, a black lacquer canister of wooden matches, and a pair of scissors.

-You want some tea? said Violet, moving from the living room to her kitchen. She filled a kettle with water from the tap and set it on the stove.

Pushing through a curtain of plastic beads, she headed into her dark bedroom. She bent over a pair of fat candles and lit them with a match. Wispy ropes of smoke trailed helically from the tip of each candle flame toward the ceiling. In the flickering light he could see hardened wax pooled on the bare wood at the base of the candles.

Violet had no bed, but slept on a futon which she pulled now from between the shadows of a wobbly armoire and a bookcase constructed of cinder blocks and planks of scrap wood. Her window was large and uncurtained, and looked out over a short, unkempt hedge along the street below. The window allowed large squares of lemony streetlight into the small room to stretch across the varnished floor. Adorning the pale walls were three large unframed posters, reproductions of famous works of abstract art. Guy arranged himself nervously on the futon while Violet went into to the kitchen, summoned by the crescendoing whistle of the kettle.

Violet returned to the bedroom carrying two large cups.

-Here, she said, offering one of them to Guy. He took it with both hands, and she sat opposite him on the floor with crossed legs. Guy placed his cup down and watched with dizzy interest the steam curl toward the ceiling. He leaned forward and breathed deeply, trying to identify the curious but not unpleasant tea scent.

-It's not really for drinking, she said, shifting her legs

to better distribute her weight. -I like to soak my fingers in it.

-What kind of tea is it?

-Different herbs. I read about it in a book.

He tested the temperature of the tea with the little finger of his right hand. Finding it not uncomfortably hot, he arranged his hands around the rim of the cup so that his fingertips were immersed in the fragrant liquid.

-Very relaxing, he declared.

She smiled her crooked smile.

-Cigarette? She did not wait for his reply but lit for herself a filterless cigarette from a half-crushed pack lying on the floor. In the light from the flaring match Guy could see that her hands shook slightly.

-You shouldn't smoke, he said equably.

-You think? She exhaled a lungful of blue smoke. The smoke spiraled in a lazy stream upwards, twining with the steam from the tea, and flowered in layers in the still air.

A moment of silence passed between them.

She sat down cross-legged, dipped the fingers of her left hand into the tea, and playfully flicked her hand at Guy. He felt drops of the hot liquid on his face but made no motion to wipe them away. Violet sighed, dropped her cigarette into the cup, and stood up. She fumbled with the zipper of her heavy black pants. She stepped out of the pants and came toward him. Leaning back on his elbows and peering in the candlelight at her face, Guy saw that her eyes were bright, glittering with unshed tears.

She bent forward, and Guy saw on the candlelit wall her shadow lean into his. The two shadows appeared to kiss, and he closed his eyes but did not feel the pressure of her lips. When he opened his eyes again she was staring at him from a distance of six inches. He could feel her breath, quick and warm, and her hair had fallen forward so that lank strands brushed his cheekbones.

-You've always been so nice to me, she murmered in his ear.

-I'm a nice person.

-*Love is not love which alters when it alteration finds*, she said. -*Or bends with the remover to remove.*

-You're left-handed, Guy observed, weakly, irrelevantly.

-I'm left-handed, she agreed, then kissed each of his eyelids. -And you're probably the first person since my high school art teacher to notice that.

-Okay, he said.

22. BILLY DESCRIBES HIS FIRST ENCOUNTER WITH THE MOPED MARAUDERS, APPROXIMATELY TWO WEEKS BEFORE THE KOREAN CHECK-CASHING FIASCO

So I'm out walking the dogs . . .

-You mean dragging the dogs behind your car, said Guy.

-Don't interrupt. This is serious. There's a gang of moped riders that go around terrorizing innocent drivers.

-Okay, I'll bite. What's the punch line?

-It's not a joke! I wish it was a joke. They go around in a pack of like ten. It's not just cars, it's pedestrians and especially, especially bicyclists. They're sworn enemies of Critical Mass.

-The who what?

-You know, that organization of bike riders that's trying to make the city more bike-friendly. The Moped Marauders hate them most of all. They're led by this one redheaded girl with a tourmaline-colored moped with matching helmet. The others ride different colors but everyone matches—helmet and bike. The leader, though, the redhead . . .

-Is she cute?

-Well, yeah, she would be if she wasn't evil. They surrounded me and started calling me names. Threatened to call the ASPCA on me.

-Which, you may recall, is not the first time someone's threatened to do that.

-But I knew you'd never follow through. These guys, though, totally different story. They mean business.

-By the way, where did you learn the word "tourmaline"?

-The redhead corrected me when I called her moped green. See what I'm saying? She's evil.

-I can see that. So what did you do?

-I pulled over and pretended to call 911.

-You don't have a cell phone.

-That's why I pretended. They saw right through that, though, so I just rolled up the windows and waited them out. Eventually they got bored and went away. I think they saw a bike rider.

-Sounds pretty random.

-If by "random" you mean "incredibly dangerous and potentially life-threatening," then I agree.

-Okay.

-Hey, you want to play *Guitar Hero III?*

-Again?

-Yes, again.

-Are you going to be Nikki Simp?

-You can be Nikki Simp if you want, said Billy with a distinct lack of enthusiasm.

-I'm kidding. I have no idea why anyone would want to be Nikki Simp.

-Umm, because she totally rocks?

-There. You said it again.

-Said what?

-*She.* You want to be a girl.

-I don't want to be a girl. I want to be Nikki Simp. And I don't really want to *be* Nikki Simp, I just want to pretend.

-This is like one step away from cross-dressing.

-It's a video game, Guy.

-Whatever, Ed Wood.

23. GUY AND VIOLET RESPLENDENT IN THE FULMINANT GLORY OF THEIR LOVE, LYING ON THE BED IN VIOLET'S APARTMENT THE ONE NIGHT SHE TOOK HIM TO HER APARTMENT, FIVE OR POSSIBLY SIX DAYS BEFORE THE KOREAN CHECK-CASHING FIASCO

Had we but world enough, and time, I'd explain the starry sky into a glass of wine we both could drink, and understand.

–You're an ass.

–There's a difference between borrowing and stealing.

–It's not my ambition to be some kind of gangster's moll. You're not Clyde. I'm definitely not Bonnie. Stealing and killing don't turn me on.

–I can start with a line from Marvell, but if I change its meaning and context, and finish it with an original thought of my own, that's borrowing. What's the phrase? *Genius borrows, less-than-genius steals.* Obviously that's a paraphrase.

–The odds of you getting caught are extremely high. Especially with Billy.

–What's wrong with Billy?

–You mean besides the fact he's an idiot?

–Okay.

-Okay *what*, okay?

-Okay, yes, he's an idiot. But he's not a drunk, or a junkie, or . . . He's a good kid. He's just . . . he gets things mixed up.

-At least a junkie's motivated. At least a junkie has to learn how to be smart, to steal without getting caught.

-Billy will be fine. It's not like he actually has to do anything.

-Billy not doing anything doesn't scare me. Billy doing something scares me. And he's perfectly capable of doing something. That's the problem.

-That's one of the problems. The other is you simply don't trust me.

-I trust you with some things. I don't trust you with this.

-But the definition of love is trust. Mutual trust.

-The definition of love, Guy, is love.

-Why won't you marry me?

-Because you're not serious. And if you were serious I wouldn't hang out with you.

-I'm serious as a kitten with a beach ball.

-You need to call off this stupid plan.

-Too late. Wheels are in motion. As we speak, there are literally wheels turning.

-If you don't call it off I might be forced to take drastic action.

-All action is drastic. It's just a question of timing.

-And you're incapable of taking anything seriously. Because you're afraid.

-I suppose that's true. But I don't suppose it matters.

-Why?

-Because I can't do anything about it.

24. BILLY EXPLAINS TO GUY, SITTING IN THE BAR, THE ABSENCE OF GREGORY, WHO WAS SUPPOSED TO MEET THEM AT THE BAR, WHICH HE MANAGES, TO DISCUSS DRIVING THE GETAWAY CAR, THREE DAYS BEFORE THE KOREAN CHECK-CASHING FIASCO

It's complicated. He thinks his wife and daughter have been replaced by imposters.

-Have they?

-I think that's something only Gregory would know.

-Because he's the only one who knows them well enough.

-There's that too.

-Okay, you're holding something back.

-Gregory's an enlightened person. He has . . . certain insights.

-Insights.

-He's connected to higher energies than you and me. He gets messages. Important messages. Save-the-planet kind of important.

-Gregory has information that can save the planet.

-I believe that to be possible.

-You believe anything to be possible. You're a believer. Your name should be Believee, The Boy Who Believes.

–I'm credulous, it's true. I don't think that's necessarily bad.

–Of course you don't. Believee. Note that down somewhere for a T-shirt idea. We need more T-shirt ideas. *The Boy Who Believes.*

–He's got these wedding photos he carries around, and then some current photos, and he makes you look at both sets, and he won't let up until you agree that the woman in the current photos is clearly a duplicate. And really, by the time you're done looking, it seems somehow . . . plausible.

–What's the thinking behind this?

–What do you mean?

–Well, why would someone replace his family with imposters?

–I think he thinks it's to distract him from his mission.

–I thought his mission was to drive the getaway car for us.

–Not that mission.

–Although I'm starting to think we could find a better candidate.

–He's an excellent driver.

–Are you trying to be funny?

–I don't think so.

–Okay. Well, the world is full of excellent drivers. Some of these might not even be entirely insane. How about let's say we look for one of those.

–I'd like to give Gregory a chance.

–We gave Gregory a chance. And from what you've told me, I really don't think it'd be fair to distract him any further from his save-the-planet mission. Or his find-his-real-family mission. Either of those two are more important than helping us rob a check-cashing place.

-This will not make Gregory happy.

-I don't mean to seem callous, but I think Gregory's got bigger problems. I think he's got a long way to go in the direction of happiness before he can even call himself depressed. My mom always told me that you can't depend on someone else for your own happiness. We'd be doing him a favor, Billy. And more importantly, we'd be doing *us* a favor. We don't do enough favors for us, in my opinion.

-Maybe you're right.

-You understand this isn't really about Gregory.

-I guess.

-I'm sure Gregory is a great guy.

-Yes.

-He runs a nice bar, even if it's a little too clean.

-He does! Plus he's figured out a way to construct a supercomputer using enormous crystals.

-Of course he has.

-More like a spiritual computer, but still based on science. Something to do with a quantum mechanic.

-You mean quantum mechanics?

-He made it sound like there was only one.

-You should really be talking to Marcus about all this.

-Oh, sure. He'd just dismiss me as a crackpot.

-I doubt he'd actually use the word "crackpot." That's not a word you hear very often in conversation.

-Well, whatever word you use to dismiss someone with a possibly insanely great idea but which you don't believe is insanely great, but maybe only insane . . . that's the word he would use. You know I'm right.

-Anyway—and I would never demean you by calling you a crackpot, by the way, whatever else you want to say about me I offer equal time to all points of view—quantum

mechanics is probably not going to help us in this particular situation.

–Okay.

–I might know a man who can drive the getaway car.

–Who is it?

–Some guy I met at a party a few weeks ago.

–Who is it?

–A guy who's proved himself extremely helpful to me
in many ways, most of which would be tedious to iterate
now. He seems okay. He's not worried about his family being replaced with sinister doubles. He doesn't collect crystals. He knows how to drive. He even has a car. And . . . I
get the impression he wouldn't mind participating in some
well-paid criminal activity.

–What's his name?

–That reminds me of a joke. Two would-be Islamic terrorists crash a flaming jeep full of gas canisters into an airport
in Scotland. Due to a combination of incompetence and luck,
the canisters fail to fully ignite. One of the blokes gets oot the
jeep, on fire, and starts throwing punches at the cops.

–How is that a joke? Didn't it actually happen?

–That part's not the joke. You're too impatient. Anyway,
they found out the names of the fellows what done it.

–Weren't they actually doctors or something?

–Stop. Just stop. Forget what may or may not have happened in what you like to call "real life."

–Okay. Sorry. Go on.

–You've made it almost impossible.

–I'm . . .

–I said *almost*. Stop talking. Okay, so, they found out the
names of them as what done the job: Sinjdin Majeep and
Maheed Zaroastin.

-That's weird you would say "them as what done the job." That's not American phrasing.

-Of course it's not. I'm setting up a Scottish joke. A joke that only people who are familiar with British phrasing would find funny, and even then many would find in poor taste at best, completely irresponsible, racist, and unfunny at worst.

-Okay, so when's the joke?

-I did the joke.

-I don't get it.

-*Sinjdin Majeep and Maheed Zaroastin.*

-Means nothing to me.

-Okay. Good.

-You're not going to explain it?

-No, I'm not, Billy. Life is already too long as it is. I don't want to make it any longer.

-Name of the driver.

-I said I wasn't going to . . .

-No, not in the joke. The man you met at the party.

-Oh. Right. His name is Sven.

25. THE TRUTH ABOUT VIOLET, AS RELUCTANTLY DISCLOSED BY THE NOT ENTIRELY OMNISCIENT BUT VERY RELIABLE NARRATOR, STEPPING OUT OF THE FRAME OF THE STORY FOR AN INSTANT

In India, women of a certain caste whose husbands die are forced to remain in mourning for the rest of their lives. They're no longer allowed to wear makeup or jewelry. They're made to shave their heads and wear only white. Their shadows are considered bad luck. Eventually, many of them end up in a particular city—whose name I forget since having read the CNN article—where they can at least congregate and take comfort from their own accursed kind. This place is called the City of Widows.

Violet is a widow. True, she killed her husband, but it was an accident, and though she did not love him she was sorry for having caused his death. Most of her actions in the five years since can be seen as a kind of American version of the City of Widows. Call it the City of Windows: Violet became a flagrant and habitual exhibitionist, a willing slave to the erotic whimsies of the Nation of Men, not because she enjoyed it, but because she decided—whether consciously or subconsciously is not the issue—that if she were not to be paired with one man only she would be paired with all men generally. She decided that she would, in the words of one of her favorite pop songs, fuck the pain away.

You can't fuck the pain away, of course. Like all successful pop songs, the central conceit is a beautiful lie. But you can try, and Violet tried. She had been married for five years, and unmarried now for the same, but in her mind still married, still unable to sleep in a shared bed unshared. Five years of practice had unprepared Violet for solitude.

Her old apartment too, impossible. Every inch imprinted with the presence of the dead man, corners of rooms and even cobwebs brushed with faint breath. It can all go to hell. The plants can die from neglect, now. Framed photos smothered under dust. Now. What energy's left she summoned to wake, and walk, and fuck. All else is definition of useless. Scrape remains of food into crammed trashcan, pile dish onto pile of dishes in sink. She used to be tidy. Now she's only ever tired. Any help sleep provides removed by the reeling void of waking up alone, without light or heat or right, in darkness made still darker by indifferent empty space. The void, of course, merely Violet's stomach grumbling from hunger. Empty is as empty does.

Shame. What you feel when you're not afraid. Rare's the peace that preempts either, rarer still the feathery tickle of contentment (that is to say happiness, Violet, don't be shy, a thing does not disappear from earth just because it disappears from your own little life). We ought to be better learned of the selfishness of gentlemen: the oblique glances, the question-mark eyebrows, appetites to sate, egos to salve: enervation itself.

The last thing dies in a woman is hope. Even unreasonable fancy, in place of hope. One jar in the back of the malodorous fridge, never opened. A token but of what. Symbolic but of what. The jar labeled *Jam*, the label hand-lettered, unspecified as to flavor or provenance or date of purchase. As long as she can remember, that jar has sat. Absorbed the passing of time as a process of refilling. Violet likes to think that sealed in the jar are the years. Time itself, gone bad.

26. BILLY, STRANDED ON A HILL-SIDE BY GUY, HAS AN UNFORTUNATE ENCOUNTER, LESS THAN AN HOUR AFTER THE KOREAN CHECK-CASHING FIASCO

Billy stood for a few moments staring in disbelief at the top of the hillside where Guy had just gotten into his stolen Mini Cooper and sped off at an unsafe speed up the treacherous curves of Larkin Heights.

-Well, that's just fine, he said to no one. -That's just fucking fine.

He began scooping up the scattered bills Guy had flung willy-nilly into the brush. A small shower of rocks fell from an outcropping directly above Billy, hitting him on the head.

-Ow! he exclaimed, peering to the heavens. -Haven't you done enough for one day?

Which is when he saw the mountain lion, standing on the outcropping not ten feet above, eyeing him with more than casual interest, and growling ominously.

-I guess not, murmured Billy.

The mountain lion crouched, then jumped, and landed directly on top of Billy. Snarls from the animal and high-pitched yelps from Billy ensued, along with a fair amount of desperate flailing of limbs.

At that moment, higher on the hill, a pair of backpackers paused in their climb to stare at the commotion below. One of them whipped out a camcorder.

-Shouldn't we, you know, try to help? asked the nonfilming hiker.

-After I get this. We can throw rocks at him, scare him away. Looks like he's just toying with the guy anyway.

Billy fought with the mountain lion for what seemed to him like an eternity. He could see blood dripping down one of his arms. Billy had always been scared at the sight of blood, but he was now past the point of phobia. He was fighting for his life. Out of the corner of his eye, he saw one of the rocks that had tumbled down from the outcropping as the mountain lion approached. He stretched his bloody arm to its limit, and grabbed hold of the rock. With all his remaining strength, he bashed the mountain lion on the nose with it. The mountain lion was neither fazed nor amused, and furthermore Billy's balance had been affected by bashing the mountain lion with the rock. He fell backwards, and landed headfirst with a considerable thud.

-Huh, said Billy, still holding the rock, still dripping with blood, just before crumpling to the ground and losing consciousness.

The two backpackers came scrambling down the hill.

-Hey, man, are you okay? said the nonfilming one.

-You're in the frame! said the one with the camcorder. -Move!

Billy stirred into consciousness. -What happened? he asked.

-I don't know. The mountain lion just sort of pawed and sniffed at you and then went away. Maybe he figured you were dead.

-I think I need to go to a hospital, said Billy, now in a state of shock, covered in scratches, bruises, and bleeding from several open wounds.

-Can you walk? asked the nonfilming backpacker.

-I don't know.

-We'll help you. It's not far to Larkin General.

-Sweet! said the backpacker with the camcorder. -Put your arm around him and help him up the hill. I'm gonna get the whole thing. Dude, you're gonna be a YouTube star!

-Okay, said Billy.

27. WHAT VIOLET SAID TO CHARLIE, FOUR DAYS BEFORE THE CHECK-CASHING FIASCO, IN THE BACK ROOM OF THE KOREAN CHECK-CASHING PLACE, AFTER HOURS

You understand this is just a one-time thing, Charlie.

-I understand.

-And that I'm not actually attracted to you or anything. Strictly speaking, this is a bargain. I fuck you, and you fuck Guy and Billy. The first fuck is meant literally, the second metaphorically.

-I understand.

-We're not going to see each other ever again after this. Or probably not anyway. Life is strange.

-I understand.

-Don't you even want to know why I want to screw up Guy's plan to rob your store?

-No.

-And you don't care about losing your share of the money?

-No.

Violet considered Charlie's answers for a moment.

-Not good enough, she finally replied.

-What's not good enough?

-Why don't you want to know anything about my motivations? It suggests to me that you don't have any intention of following through with Guy's plan, and that for me to fuck you would just be . . . superfluous.

-I don't know what that means.

-It means you're a creep. But that's not important. I figured you for a creep. I didn't figure you for an untrustworthy creep.

-I'm trustworthy.

-So you intend to follow through with this ridiculous and almost-certain-to-fail plan to rob your check-cashing place?

-I do. Or I did. Until now. Why do you think it's almost certain to fail? Guy's got everything worked out.

-Yeah, he's good at that. He's also good at the *gang aft agley* part about best-laid schemes. I mean in the original Burns poem, not the Steinbeck version.

Charlie gave a look expressing puzzlement.

-Don't even bother, she continued, before Charlie could protest. -I don't know why I'm talking to you like this. I think I might actually be nervous. Which is odd. I'm almost never nervous.

-Maybe you actually care about him?

-Yeah, replied Violet softly, surprising herself at her own half-admission. -I . . . it's just with Guy, he's always got these grand projects, he's so busy trying to make something out of nothing that he can't see the something he already . . . Anyway, I want him to be happy. I want to try to make him happy. I don't do this, as a rule. I don't get involved. That's how my husband got killed.

She reacted to Charlie's shocked expression with an impatient toss of her head.

-If he goes through with the plan—which I did my best to talk him out of, but to be honest my best is not very good, so I kind of figured he wouldn't listen—he will get caught, or worse, and from what I understand, your part in all this is central, so if you don't do your part, he will still fail, but on a much smaller scale. Call it damage control.

-Damage control, repeated Charlie.

A moment of heavy silence passed between them. Violet sighed.

 -Am I really that beautiful?

-Yes.

-Okay, then. Let's get started. She began undressing.

-No, said Charlie.

Violet stopped. -No? You're saying no?

-Yes.

Violet shrugged, began dressing again. -So much for Plan Violet.

-It wasn't a very good plan.

-You're probably right, said Violet, in a slow monotone.

28. DAY OF THE LOCUS. GUY AND BILLY SIT IDLING IN THEIR PROBABLY STOLEN CAR IN THE PARKING LOT OF THE KOREAN CHECK-CASHING PLACE

What time is it? asked Billy.

–It's thirty seconds later than the last time you asked me.

–I forget what time you told me it was then.

–That's not my problem. I'll let you know when it's time.

–Are we close?

–We're not far.

–Do you think Sven should be here by now?

–No, but I'm beginning to have doubts about you being here.

–I'd feel better going in if I knew our getaway driver had arrived.

–I told him to get here at 9:05. We're going in at exactly nine. We've been over this, Billy, and over this and over this.

–I know. I guess you could say I'm skittish.

–Turns out.

-Can we go over procedure one last time?

-I'd prefer not to.

Guy turned to Billy, a wan smile on his face.

-William. Look around. There are dozens of cars here, same as us, engines idling, same as us. That's why we picked this day. Everyone's here waiting for the place to open, pay-checks or Social Security checks in hand. There's nothing suspicious in us being here as well. And, if you must know, although I haven't said anything, Sven is already here. I'm not going to point him out until we're on our way out of the store, because if I do you'll be constantly looking over at him, which is the type of thing we really don't need right now.

-He's here? Where? Billy's head spun around, looking.

-I was kidding. He's not here.

-I'd feel better if he was here.

Guy looked at his watch, sighed. Glancing into the store, he could see Charlie at the front door, beginning the process of unlocking the series of deadbolts. People began to exit their cars and make their way to the door.

-Okay. It's time.

-It's time? Already?

-Yes, already. Let's have the ski masks.

Billy unfurled the crumpled paper bag in his lap, put his hand in, extracted two knit ski caps, robin's-egg blue in color.

-What the fuck? said Guy.

-What?

-Were they out of hot pink?

-You didn't say what color. These were on clearance.

-Do you know why they were on clearance? Because they're incredibly garish and ugly. Which is kind of beside the point, because I'm not criticizing your fashion sense, Billy, I'm criticizing your common sense.

-The security camera is black-and-white.

-Even if you know that to be true, and I don't see how, unless you believe everything you see on TV, that's not the point. The point is, we are now readily identifiable. We are the baby-blue bandits. All of the eyewitnesses to this crime will now remember one very specific detail: the color of our ski masks.

-Can I make a point?

-I think you've already made enough points for one lifetime.

-Here's my thinking, for what it's worth: yes, they'll remember our ski masks. But that's *all* they'll remember. Because the masks are so memorable, they'll fail to take note of any other salient characteristics, like height, skin tone, girth . . .

-Girth?

-I could stand to lose a little weight. Around the middle. Look, we ditch the ski masks first chance we get, and there's nothing to tie us to the job. Everyone's out looking for the . . . what you said, the baby-blue bandits, and we're no longer any kind of blue.

-Are you just turning a negative into a positive, or did you actually think of this beforehand?

-Little bit of both, actually. I don't favor analysis as much as you do.

-Right. Okay. You ready?

-I'm nervous as hell, frankly.

-Me too. Let's go.

29. THE LAST TIME GUY'S MOM AND DAD ATE AT THE PINE CLUB, THE NIGHT BEFORE THE KOREAN CHECK-CASHING FIASCO, ALBEIT A COUPLE OF THOUSAND MILES AWAY

Should have seen the look on his face. I'm telling you.
-I'm sure it was something.

-You bet it was something. I told that fucker . . .

-Language . . .

-Oh, fuck the fucking language. I'm celebrating. You know how much commission I get off this deal?

-You're always celebrating, dear. There are other people in this restaurant. It's a public place.

-Yeah, whatever, okay. But you should have seen it.

-I'm sure it was something.

-You're sure it was . . . Do you even listen to me when I'm talking?

-I'm sorry.

-This is a big day for me. Wouldn't hurt you to pay some goddamn attention when I'm talking.

-I said I was sorry.

Guy's mom drifted back into her reverie. The usual one: where she'd made a different choice, thirty-five years ago, and was now in Buenos Aires running a small, secondhand, English-language bookstore. There weren't many customers, but enough, and her Spanish had acquired sufficient polish that she was able to order food at the local markets without embarrassment, and in any case was well-known enough to the vendors that before she even arrived at their stall they'd have laid out exactly the sort of thing she imagined they imagined she'd want. She'd go back to her small apartment above the bookstore and cook dinner for herself, fresh vegetables and fish, nothing fancy, and watch the sun set on her balcony, the heat shimmering on the periphery of her vision as she paged idly through a recent best seller about a man having a heart attack in a steak restaurant in Dayton, Ohio . . .

–Robert? she asked, seeing the odd expression on his face, just after he dropped his steak knife with a soundless clatter in the suddenly silent restaurant.

This is strange, she thought. This is both part of and apart from my fantasy.

Her husband clutched at his chest and mouthed with great effort some words. Were the words meant for her?

–For. Fuck. Sake. The words popped one by one like little balloons in the air. Experiments have been done on this, she thought. I remember reading. If you take the words out of the ambient noise they lose all meaning. Then if you add back the noise, the words make sense.

The noise came back. The rush of concerned voices from the surrounding booths felt to Laura like a physical blow, like the face slap that Robert had never once administered, not even close, their entire life together.

She watched as her husband slumped in his seat, gasping for breath and clawing at the table as he fell.

-Robert! she exclaimed, and hurried to his side just in time to catch his head in her hands before it hit the wooden floor.

Her husband was muttering something through a thin foam of blood and spittle. She leaned close to hear.

-Should have seen his fucking face, mumbled Robert.

Tears were streaming down Laura's cheeks. -I should have, Robert, I should have seen his face. I should have seen anyone's face but yours, right now, like this. I'm not ready.

-No one's ever ready, whispered Robert weakly. -I'm not ready. But you'll be all right.

-Shut up! she shrieked, uncharacteristically. Aspirin, she thought. Mrs. Sanderson said she read somewhere. Laura scrabbled desperately through her purse, clutched at a plastic bottle. Advil. Does that have the same . . . ?

She tried to shove two red pills into her husband's mouth, but he had lost consciousness. A young man identified himself as a doctor, bent over Robert's body. Laura stepped away and sank back down in her seat, dazed.

The ceremony was beautiful, she thought. I never expected Guy to show up, but he did, and Marcus and Constance, and the Sandersons, and everyone from Robert's work, and the priest gave a lovely eulogy or homily or whatever it was that priests did at a funeral, a proper Catholic burial, the plot at St. Anne's long ago chosen, a shady corner of the quiet cemetery. Except that St. Anne's had been razed to make way for a parking structure.

-I'm afraid it's too late, said the young doctor, quietly, taking Laura's hand in his, a practiced move.

-Too late for what? she asked.

30. SQUIRREL VS. CAT: A DISCUSSION IN THE PROBABLY STOLEN CAR BETWEEN GUY AND BILLY IN THE PARKING LOT OF THE KOREAN CHECK-CASHING PLACE, ONE HOUR BEFORE THE KOREAN CHECK-CASHING FIASCO

L et me ask you a question: who do you think would win in a fight between a squirrel and a cat? said Guy

-Depends on the cat, obviously, said Billy. -But in general the cat. I had a cat once, used to kill squirrels and bring them back to the house, as presents, or trophies or something . . .

-I don't mean a regular fight. I mean if the squirrel was on a skateboard and had a little helmet on, like a Roman centurion's helmet except squirrel-size. And you pushed the skateboard squirrel toward the cat, who was maybe asleep. And you filmed the whole thing on a camcorder and posted it on a website.

-Which website?

-You're missing the point. It's like the difference between a Francophone and a Francophile. The former can speak French, the latter loves France, or the French or anything and everything to do with French culture.

-I didn't know you spoke French.

-I don't. I pronounce French. It's the same with Russian. I know the Cyrillic alphabet and I'm told my Russian accent is very good, but I don't know what a single word means. Well, I know one or two, but not much beyond "hello" and "goodbye."

-So you could read an entire page of a Russian book out loud in the original . . .

-And not know the meaning of even one sentence. But if I were reading to an audience of native speakers, they'd understand perfectly. I can also do this with Latin and ancient Greek. It's an unusually useless talent.

-I kind of like that.

-Who wouldn't? You're starting to see things my way.

-I am. I admit it.

-That's very gratifying.

-I really wish we didn't have to go through with this, sighed Billy.

-Your wishes are the engine that will drive this economy out of its present recession.

-I'm not sure that's true, but thanks.

-You always read about these crazy revolutionary ideas that were funded by eccentric millionaires . . .

-Or billionaires . . .

-I tell you what, and you can have this idea for free after Pandemonium takes off: someone should start a site that lists names and contact info of eccentric millionaires.

-And billionaires.

-It might be harder to get the proper information with billionaires. Especially eccentric ones. I have a feeling they're probably pretty reclusive.

-Like Howard Hughes.

-Well, I mean, he's like the summa of eccentric billionaires. In the movie *The Plane Magnate*, the actor who played Hughes invested him with a number of tics, even as a young man. He had some form of obsessive-compulsive disorder, clearly.

-For which they have medications now.

-They have medications for everything. That's why everyone's so ordinary.

-Do you think so?

-Don't get me wrong. I'm not anti-meds. At this very moment I'm on two different kinds of antianxiety medicine.

-Wow.

-Yes—but this is important—medications are only useful when abused. Drugs are only any good to anyone when you take too many or too much of one kind; in other words, when you derive some pleasure from them. Otherwise . . . what's the point?

-I'm sure there are some people who really do need them. You know, to function.

-Function? Why function? Who needs more functioning human beings? It's really quite astounding, if you ask me, the sheer quantity of *normal* in the world today. I think that's the real horror of modern life.

-All the more reason for Pandemonium.

-You know, it's funny. Just when I think you don't understand anything I'm saying, ever, you say something that shows you understand perfectly.

-I'm glad you think so.

-If only more people had your attitude. Not everyone, obviously, because we need and have always needed a certain number of normals. But ye gods! You walk down the street—okay, you don't walk down the street, because nobody walks down the street in Los Angeles, obviously, that was a cliché even before it was a ridiculous New Wave pop song by a terrible New Wave band—but you go somewhere like a shopping mall where there's just tons of people, and what do you see?

-Shopping.

-Shopping. Exactly. Most normal thing in the world. Crowds of normals bunched together like blood cells, moving in rhythm to some great bio-mechanical heart under the streets or up in the sky.

-Hard to say where the heart lies.

-What is that, poetry?

-I don't think so.

-You should start writing down everything you say. Sometimes you say things that could be construed as, I don't know, aphoristic.

-Aphoristic?

-At worst gnomic. Gnomic is always good because rarely will you get called on it. People are too scared to admit they might not understand what you're saying. The normals, I mean.

-Did you just start calling them normals?

-Pretty much.

-Good. Because I don't remember you using that word before and I was worried about losing my mind.

-As you do.

-Well, everyone worries about losing his mind at some point, don't they?

-No. No they don't. And to think I was beginning to trust you.

-You don't trust me? said Billy, eyeing Guy incredulously.

-I do. I do trust you. Except when I don't. Which, and don't get angry, is sometimes.

-Sometimes you don't trust me. Why?

-It's hard to put into words.

-No it's not, Guy. I know why you don't trust me.

-You do.

-It's because I'm black.

-It's . . . wow.

-Admit that you don't trust me because I'm black.

-Well, if you're going to back me into a corner like that, okay. I don't trust you because a) you're an incompetent, idiotic, untrustworthy fuck-up, and b) you actually believe you're black.

-I am. I'm part African American.

-Which part? Your lungs? Your kidneys? Because it's not an exteriorly obvious part. You're pale as any English rose.

-Skin color has nothing to do with it. Black is an outlook.

-In your case it would seem to be an overlook.

-That's you being racist.

-It's me being not insane, Billy. Just because we hired a black president, it does not mean every citizen of this nation gets to call himself black. It doesn't work that way.

-Your racism colors everything you say. Pun intended.

-If I were you I wouldn't advertise that pun.

-You're saying it was a bad pun.

-Yes.

-You're saying that African Americans are no good at puns.

-That's precisely what I'm saying, if by "African Americans" you mean "you, and you only," and by "puns" you mean "that last really bad pun."

-I won't let you box me in.

-Okay.

-I'm saying you can't box me in.

-I get it. Are you trying to write a song?

-Why? You don't think I could write a song?

-I never gave it much thought, honestly.

-By your tyrannical European standards of harmony and the well-tempered piano and so on . . .

-You don't even know what well-tempered means.

-. . . But by the rhythmic innovations of my forebears . . .

-Are you descended from bears?

-What?

-I thought you just said you're descended from bears.

-Why would I say that?

-I'm just saying what I thought you said. I'm not inside your head. I don't know why you say half the things you say.

-Are any humans descended from bears?

-I don't think so. Maybe. I'm not a scientist.

-That would be pretty neat, don't you think?

-Neat? Hell yeah, it would be neat.

-We might still have some residual bear characteristics. Like maybe that's why I like salmon so much.

-I've never seen you eat salmon.

-You've never seen me eat anything but burritos, practically. That's a question of affordability, not taste.

-Okay. So you like salmon?

-I love salmon. It's probably my favorite kind of seafood.

-You better trim your claws.

-What?

-I'm just saying, watch out for those things. If you have

residual bear characteristics. That would probably manifest in extremely fast-growing, sharp fingernails. You could cut yourself.

Billy examined his fingernails carefully. -They do grow fast.

-You see?

Billy flashed his teeth at Guy, who recoiled in horror.

-Why would you do that? asked Guy.

-Did you see anything fanglike?

-I'm actually blind now.

-Seriously.

-Seriously, I didn't look and I'm not going to look. This is why God invented the mirror.

-I don't trust mirrors.

-Of course you don't.

-Say what you want, but I don't think a mirror gives you a good idea of what you look like.

-Compared with . . .

-Compared with reality.

-How would you go about measuring something like that?

-It's like, when you look in the mirror, you get a different picture of yourself than when you see yourself on videotape or something. Because in the mirror you only look directly at yourself. But no one else sees you that way.

-So in your opinion, film or videotape is a more reliable metric for self-evaluation.

-Umm . . . yes?

-I don't know. There's so many variables in both areas, but I do see your point.

-That's all I ask.

-Lighting, film stock, exposure, on the one hand, not to mention the nearly limitless possibilities offered by digital manipulation of the image, whether moving or still. But the mirror thing . . . I do see your point. Plus, there's no way of really knowing whether the mirror isn't skewed in some way, like maybe it has an almost imperceptible flaw that produces a disproportionate distortion in the reflection. An unintentional funhouse mirror.

-That's as well as I could put it.

-Actually, it's much better than you could put it. But I think you meant it as a compliment and so I will take it as a compliment. Gracefully. With a graceful shrug that indicates both acknowledgment and gratitude. Without overdoing either.

-That sounds really . . .

-Articulate? Thank you, said Guy.

-I like your thinking.

-What does that mean, *I like your thinking?*

-What do you mean, what does it mean? It means what I said: I like your thinking.

-Score one for you on the tote board.

-What's a tote board? asked Billy.

-Maybe just a dry-erase board, which could then be configured for multiple uses.

-Can I ask you a question: are my eyes too far apart?

-What do you mean?

-I feel like my eyes are too far apart. Like weirdly so. Billy stared at his face carefully in the mirror on the passenger-side sun visor. -Wide-set eyes look untrustworthy, I think. To girls, especially, he continued.

-There's also the fact that you're a compulsive liar, replied Guy.

Billy kept staring in the mirror. -No, I don't think that's it, he said after a while.

31. GUY AND VIOLET DO DRUGS ON VIOLET'S BED, THE ONE NIGHT GUY WAS ALLOWED IN VIOLET'S APARTMENT, FIVE DAYS BEFORE THE KOREAN CHECK-CASHING FIASCO

She handed him the crumpled and perforated tinfoil, in the center of which was smeared "the dark blood of the opium," as Guy liked to call the sticky brown tar that Violet had developed a serious habit of consuming, and which Guy felt duty-bound, as a way of protecting her from herself, to share.

He held his lighter under the foil and breathed the smoke. This stuff has no effect on me, he thought, attempting to stand up and failing. I don't see the appeal.

Guy handed the foil and lighter back to Violet, who immediately took a long and deep drag.

–Good stuff, she said, exhaling.

–Yeah. So you want to go to this thing at the Gagosian?

–Not really.

–But it's your friend, right?

–I have lots of friends. And besides, remember what happened the last time we went.

Guy remembered. He remembered that if you go to the Gagosian in Beverly Hills to see a *Vanity Fair* photographer's exhibit you will encounter Damien Hirst, who does not travel light, entouragely speaking, and the exotic, swan-like Tilda Swinton, *avec mari*. Guy said let's turn off all the lights at once but Violet would not let him. I know these people, she hissed. I know people here and that would be incredibly juvenile and immature and embarrassing. Guy was not drinking the free wine because he had temporarily stopped drinking, so he didn't switch off all the lights, even though he still—to this day—believes that would have been better art than anything on display at the goddamned Gagosian.

Because, and here you have to maybe allow for Guy's immaturity and whatever Violet said, *juvenility,* but if art with a capital or even a small initial letter is meant to provoke a reaction from the spectator or audience or what-have-you—the rabble, right?—then turning out the lights when everyone is crowded together in their expensive clothes sipping cheap wine would create a small-time panic at the disco, at least, and wouldn't last very long—you could put the lights back on, since you're standing at the light switch panel in the first place, before the first ladies-in-waiting had begun to scream and the babble had barely begun to rise above a murmuration—and you could moreover walk away quickly enough from the light switches (which for future reference are right behind the stairway that leads up to the second floor) and stand a decent chance of getting away with it.

But no, this was at a time when Guy would do anything Violet asked. A time that, despite everything, never stopped existing, and will now exist forever, because Guy is in a coma, and while the best coma research sheds little insight into the actual mental processes of a comatose patient, we can assume that if Guy was in love with Violet (and despite what he would tell you, if he could speak, he was) pre-coma, then he is still in love with her now. Because he doesn't know anything that happened after he crashed through the restraining barrier, flipped over three times, and lost consciousness forever.

-You mean the nothing that happened last time we went?

-I mean the thing that would've happened if you . . . God this stuff is strong.

-Just admit you don't want to go because you'd rather stay here and get high.

-Will that make you feel better about yourself?

-Can I ask you a serious question? said Guy.

-Oh God, anything but that! Serious questions are so tedious. You know, Guy, for someone who claims to like things blurry and unstated, you're really a constructivist at heart.

-I don't suppose there's a chance you're ever wrong about anything.

-No.

At that moment, the phone in Violet's apartment rang. She leaned over to see the caller ID and groaned.

-Who? asked Guy.

-Just some guy who can't take a hint. I may have to take out a restraining order.

-You want I should, like, kick his ass?

Violet exploded with laughter that quickly turned into a coughing fit. She reached for the tinfoil and took another deep drag.

-The idea of you kicking anyone's ass. Sorry. Too funny.

-I suppose you're right. I could hire someone to do it, though. I know people.

-Oh, just leave the poor guy alone.

-Does he know about me?

-Most likely. He's kind of the obsessive type. He probably followed us here and copied your license plate and put a trace on it.

-What, he's a cop?

-No, he just knows how to do spy-type things. I don't know how. He's like some kind of tech genius. The kind who fancies himself an "artist." Which explains, I guess, his fascination with me.

-When did you dump him?

-The night I met you. Except I didn't actually dump him. We weren't going out or anything. I never even fucked him. I don't think. But you know how some guys can be . . . or maybe you don't.

-So he was there, at the Smog Cutter? What, you just left him there without telling him?

-Pretty much.

-Great. An enemy I didn't even know I had.

-He's harmless. Borderline nuts, but harmless.

-We're all borderline nuts. Borderline nuts I can handle. I just like to know when I've made a new enemy, witting or unwitting.

-What's that mean?

-It means . . . I don't know. Pass that over here, will you?

32. THE VILLAIN SVEN TRANSVOORT DESCRIBES HIS FIRST MEETING WITH GUY, SITTING COWARDLY IN HIS UNDISCLOSED LOCATION, SEVERAL WEEKS AFTER THE KOREAN CHECK-CASHING FIASCO

What's a little white lie between friends? I realize I'm assuming quite a lot, calling you my friends, but you see I have no others, just at the moment, and I could really use some.

The white lie was that Violet McKnight was my girlfriend. I am many things in addition to a sociopath, but I am not delusional, at least not in a Humbert Humbert way. I'm not anywhere near that predictable. Or, to put it the way I twittered just ten minutes ago, *I am the most interesting person you will never meet.* I thought that was rather clever, given the 140-character constraints of the form.

I was seeing her, yes, but only in the sense that one sees another person who might be described as a casual acquaintance. In fact, she was using me, or more specifically using my connections in the art world, which are really no more than a function of the money my adoptive parents left me when they died (tragically, in a car accident, which some of my new friends, that is to say you, might find ironic). My father, unlike Guy's, could never handle his liquor. And my mother didn't know how to drive. But psychoanalysis will get you nowhere, my new friends, because I did not love my parents. Or, if you like, I loved them, but in the way one loves a favorite piece of furniture or an apartment. When the furniture is stolen, or you move, you're sad at first, but you get over it fairly quickly. You don't necessarily, with parents, acquire a new piece of furniture or move into a new apartment (please try to keep up with the extended metaphor, you in the back!), but you do move on. You forget.

As for our other Forget, if Hannah Arendt was right about the banality of evil, and I see no reason to argue the point, then my subsequent encounters with Guy Forget represented probably my first encounter with pure evil. I am not equating Guy with Eichmann, I'm simply saying that had Guy been in Eichmann's place he probably would have acted similarly. He had no appetite for questioning received wisdom, no apparent talent for original thinking whatsoever. In this he was, of course, not all that different from anyone you might meet at any time in any place or especially watch run for elected office, but what distinguished Guy, what snapped my head to attention, was his self-awareness.

He walked into the after-party like he was walking onto a yacht. I should first explain that I almost never give parties in Los Angeles, not anymore. I should secondly explain that I am aware when I am paraphrasing or even stealing old song lyrics. There is intentionality to everything I say or do. There is will. There is almost always execution.

I gave this party because Violet asked me to, though

it's true I had in fact manipulated her into asking me to, because as part of my elaborate revenge plan I had "let slip" to Violet about my spurious Internet coding breakthrough, which I knew she would not fail to determine could be a useful thing for Guy to try to exploit. I pretended to give the party, therefore, under protest, with a bad attitude, determined not to have fun, determined to sulk in a corner slumped against a wall or if possible glowering in an easy chair with my legs outstretched so that people would either have to step over them or trip. As you can imagine most people tripped, because most people are incredibly unaware of their surroundings even when sober, but after two or three drinks my legs acquired the kind of invisibility I'd dreamed about as a boy.

Drunk as he was—and he was—self-absorbed and arrogant and entitled and rangy and tall and good-looking in an ordinary way, as he also was, he looked down as he approached, with a drink in both hands, and saw my legs. And stepped over them. And then turned, or gavotted, almost, and looked me directly in the eye.

This was, whether he or I knew it at that second, a crucial moment in Guy Forget's life. It was the moment I could have turned back, forgotten the elaborate revenge plan, decided he was an okay guy, or Guy, and let the whole thing drop. Instead, it was the moment that confirmed to me in the core of my being that I was doing the right thing. He should not have turned. He should not have looked me in the eye. He should have tripped over my legs like everyone else and spilled his drink, and laughed the whole thing off. Had he done so, I firmly believe, I would have let him be.

I waited a few minutes and then approached him. Almost immediately I began my well-planned counterplot, spurred on—had there been any lingering doubts in my mind before the after-party—by blind rage at his insipid manner, at the way he had of talking down to me, to *me*, whose IQ on any measurable scale towered above the collective IQ of the entire houseful of tweeting and tumbling deadheaded mannequins like the snow-capped peaks of the volcanic range of mountains in the Puy-de-Dôme serenely keeping watch over central France.

You know how sometimes you just develop an instant antipathy toward someone? Instant and unexplainable but deep and ineradicable as a vein of fool's gold in (for instance, to pick a random example) volcanic rock? That's what happened—over and above walking out of the Smog Cutter with a girl he in no way deserved, that's what provoked his end. He did enough to warrant that end, I suppose. He dug his own hole. But I filled it in.

I'm not confessing for any particular reason other than the thrill of confessing. I'm not asking for forgiveness. I'm just saying let's work out what's worth saving and what's not in this crazy two-bit town called life.

33. GUY AND BILLY DISCUSS VIOLET BEHIND HER BACK, SITTING IN THE BAR TWO DAYS BEFORE THE KOREAN CHECK-CASHING FIASCO

She'd been crying, is what I'm trying to tell you.

-She does that. Not cry, but pretend to have been crying. It's one of her most effective tools.

-You're absolutely heartless.

-Me? I'm full of heart. If my heart were any bigger we'd have to find a larger booth.

-Then why are you always putting her down?

-Listen to me, Billy. No one on this greenish-blue earth loves or cares for Violet more than I do. No one, in fact, loves or cares for her half as much as I do. I'm not really sure how you quantify loving and caring for someone, but "half as much" is not meant as a precise measurement. Don't trap me with words, Billy. I know the twists of your sophistry. You could make me believe the opposite of what I say or mean with a few well-turned questions.

-I could?

-There you go! Damn you!

-I didn't know you had such strong feelings.

-About Violet?

-About anything.

-She's misunderstood by everyone except me. I put her down out of love, you see. I don't fall for her tricks because she's better than her tricks.

-I don't know . . .

-Anything. You don't know anything. That's the Socratic method at work, old boy. Good for you. In two shakes of a lamb's tail, you'll have me believing that pornography is immoral. You're amazing!

-All I'm saying is that she's very unhappy about Plan Charlie. She doesn't want us to go through with it. And I don't like to see her unhappy. I guess I have feelings for her too.

-Of course you have feelings for her. Feelings of brotherly love, complicated by irresistible incestuous urges. We've all been there, old boy.

-Why do you keep calling me old boy?

-It's just . . . I really like that movie, *Old Boy*. And you remind me of the main character before he gets locked away in his hotel-room prison for twenty years or however long. Which, by the way, is absolutely not going to happen to you. I promise you, no matter what happens before, during, or after Plan Charlie, you will pay no price. I have carefully rigged this whole setup so that if anything goes wrong, Guy Forget and only Guy Forget will take the fall.

-What I want to know is when we get to meet this driver, this Sven dude.

-I already met him. You don't get to meet him until the day of the job.

-That makes me uncomfortable.

-I'm sorry, Billy, but surely you can see this is for your own good.

-I do see that, and I appreciate it, but it still makes me uncomfortable. I like to know the people I'm working with.

-You mean like Gregory?

-That's not fair.

-Who said anything about fair? Look, you want to meet Sven, you can meet Sven. I just don't see the point. It's an unnecessary risk, for both of you. If there was a way you could avoid seeing him on the day of the job altogether, I'd jump at it. In the meantime, the less you two know about each other, the better for both of you.

-I guess you're right.

-You guess right. I am.

-How much does Violet know about any of this?

-I have no secrets from her. I probably should, but I somehow can't. Maybe it's all the drugs. And, of course, there's you. You can't shut up about anything.

-She makes me nervous. I have to say something. I try not to talk about anything, you know, about this. I do try.

-You have a way of speaking volumes of sense amid libraries of nonsense. Some kind of freakish gift.

-She asks me all the time, but I don't tell her much. I swear. I can tell from her questions that she knows what's up.

-And she can tell from your answers what's up. It's like Mrs. Parker's vicious circle.

-You already told me you've told her everything. What's the point? I'm as discrete as I know how to be.

-I know. I'm sorry. I should give you more credit. You're a smart kid, old boy.

34. THE KOREAN CHECK-CASHING FIASCO, FINALLY, TOLD IN A STYLIZED MANNER THAT AT ONCE EVOKES AND MOCKS THE ABSURDITY OF THE SITUATION, WITHOUT STRAYING TOO FAR FROM WHAT ACTUALLY HAPPENED

They entered the store, Guy and Billy, Billy and Guy, wearing their baby-blue ski masks and brandishing obviously fake pistols, and the tellers, counting money behind their cages, barely looked up. One supposes that they see this sort of thing on a regular basis, maybe even with baby-blue ski masks. It's difficult to say, just as it was difficult to read the expression on Charlie's face as he stared at the masked duo from behind Window 3, frozen with what could be shock, but looked enough like shock that Guy actually double-checked his watch to make sure they were on the right day and time. Which of course they were. Guy went up to Charlie's cage, and in his best menacing whisper, which by the way is not very menacing, he said, "Hand over the cash in your drawer, punk."

Charlie shrugged, looked down at his drawer, and after a moment's hesitation that Guy thought, at the time, was a magnificently ad-libbed piece of acting, removed it from his register and handed it through the slot in the Plexiglas window. Obviously the drawer itself would not fit through the slot, so he started removing bundles of cash and pushing them through the slot, where Billy stuffed them into a plastic garbage bag. Which is when Guy noticed that something had obviously gone very, very wrong. There was nothing like $100,000 in Charlie's drawer. There was more like $12,000, the amount that's normally supposed to be there, but not this morning, the morning of Guy and Billy and Charlie's elaborately worked-out plan.

–What gives? Guy hissed at Charlie, who again shrugged, pushing rolls of goddamn quarters through the window by this time.

–Couldn't do it, bro, he whispered back, further infuriating Guy by the use of the word "bro."

Guy could only imagine the different shades of magenta his skin must be turning underneath his baby-blue mask.

–That's it? *Couldn't do it, bro?* Why couldn't you do it?

–Ask Violet.

–Yeah, I'd like to ask Violet, Charlie, but she ain't fucking here just at the minute, is she?

–What?

The sirens were already audible. They had at most thirty seconds to get out of there.

–We have at most thirty seconds to get out of here, Guy said to Billy, who had just finished stuffing cash into the plastic bag.

–What?

–Get out! Guy shouted, grabbing the bag from Billy and heading for the door.

35. WHAT HAPPENED NEXT WAS JUST DUMB, IN THE IMMEDIATE AFTERMATH OF THE KOREAN CHECK-CASHING FIASCO

Where's Sven? yelled Billy, racing out the door after Guy, ripping off his baby-blue ski mask.

-First of all, who told you to take off your ski mask? asked Guy. -And second of all, I don't know. He's supposed to be here. Right here. Literally right where I'm standing. In a tan Ford Mustang.

-I've never even seen a tan Mustang.

-That doesn't mean they don't exist. You've never seen God, right?

-This is your fault. You hired the driver and the driver is not here and the car is not here and now we have to take the probably stolen car, which was not, N, O, T, the plan.

-I know. I'm sorry. Can you kind of hurry, though? I'll apologize all the way to wherever we get to before the cops nail us.

-I just . . . You always do that, and it lowers my self-esteem. Which is not good for my self-esteem.

At which point three police cars, sirens wailing, sped

past the check-cashing place without slowing down. Guy and Billy looked at each other. Guy took off his mask and shrugged.

-Now I don't know whether we're really unlucky or really lucky, said Guy.

-I'll get the car, said Billy.

36. A PRIVATE CONVERSATION BETWEEN GUY AND VIOLET, SITTING ON VIOLET'S BED THE ONE TIME HE WAS ALLOWED TO VISIT HER APARTMENT, FIVE DAYS BEFORE THE KOREAN CHECK-CASHING FIASCO

I'm strong, said Violet.
-Yes, but are you Army strong?

-I don't know. Maybe. Do you think you're book hot?

-I'm definitely not TV hot. You're like movie hot, though.

-Seriously? Do you mean indie movie hot or block-buster movie hot?

-You're right on the edge. You're maybe rising starlet hot?

-That's so sweet.

In the dark the wallpaper, bland rows of tipped pyramids on a white background, acquired a sheen of sweat. Emotional humidity. Guy had no way of stopping her. Smoke from his improperly stubbed cigarette curled upwards from the ashtray balanced on his thigh and flowered in unexpected ways near the ceiling, dissolving at length in the murk. He couldn't stop her. Her bare shoulders reflected striped moonlight onto the piled pillows. They talked for a while longer but talking only drew tighter the tense cords banding Guy's stomach. His throat clenched. He had a coughing fit and lit another cigarette. Moths beat at the window screen, alarmed at the sudden silence. Truth is, he didn't want to stop her. She opened her eyes; he saw narrow gemlike slits glitter on the moon-dappled and striated bed. The distance between her hand and his chest was negatively charged, prickly with latent energy. The angel of perception shifted; Guy turned away and leaned on a nervous elbow, watching the blue glow of her digital clock on a nearby end table register the slowly scrolling text of time.

-What are you thinking? asked Guy, after a while.

-If you have to ask, then I really don't think there's much point in me being here.

-I mean besides that. Obviously. I don't know anything about you.

Violet sat up in the bed, alarmed.

-You've never wanted to know anything about me.

-Yeah, I know. It's uncharacteristic.

-I don't tell people stuff like that.

-Okay, first: stuff like what? And second: people? I've been demoted?

-And this is one of the reasons why.

-Just forget I said anything.

-I never understand when anyone says that. You did say it. It's now part of my memory. I can't choose which memories to remember and which to forget. I wish I could. And you're telling me to forget it only doubles the chances that I'll remember it.

-It's an expression. I don't mean actually forget, but act as if you've forgotten. Pretend, in other words, I never said anything about how I don't know anything about you, and I'd like to know something, not a whole lot, but maybe where you're from, your middle name, favorite flavor of ice cream . . .

–I'm lactose-intolerant. I don't eat ice cream.

–There, see? Now I know something about you. That wasn't so difficult, was it?

–Unless I was lying. I do that a lot.

–Yeah, me too. Like, for example, when I said I was a rich Internet entrepreneur.

–I never believed that.

–It was still a lie.

–Okay.

–Truth is, I *will be* a rich Internet entrepreneur. I just need some cash to fund my prototype for this really ingenious new technology that . . . You stopped listening, didn't you?

–Uh-huh.

–Okay. Well, maybe you'll listen to this: my plan to raise the cash involves robbing a Korean check-cashing place.

Violet chuckled softly. –Right.

–Seriously. I've got a guy on the inside. Whole thing's worked out.

–Please don't do this.

–Why?

–Not that it's any of my business, but you'll get caught, you'll go to jail, and I'll have to forget, or rather pretend, that I ever knew you. Which would be a shame because you're not entirely worthless.

–This thing is foolproof.

–Is Billy involved?

–Of course Billy's involved. He's an integral part of the plan.

-Then it's not foolproof. If Billy's involved, by definition your plan is not foolproof, and you will get caught, whether immediately or eventually, and then . . . all that stuff I already said.

-You'll change your tune when I show you the money.

-There were so many clichés in that sentence I don't know whether to laugh or cry.

-How about instead we just have sex?

-Only if you promise to drop your foolproof plan. Seriously.

Guy waited an appropriate length of time, pretending to consider.

-Fine. Okay. I promise to drop the plan.

Violet unhooked her bra and threw it on the floor.

-Liar, she said, reaching for Guy's pants.

37. BILLY PITCHES PANDEMONIUM TO A NEW GROUP OF POTENTIAL INVESTORS, SEVERAL WEEKS AFTER THE KOREAN CHECK-CASHING FIASCO

So that's, like, more or less how it works.

-How what works? asked one of the investors.

-Pandemonium. I just demonstrated it.

-What do you mean?

-When you clicked on that website, you got advertised to. Or however you want to say it.

-What was the ad for?

-Ah. Yes. For demonstration purposes, I chose a public service announcement regarding dental hygiene. Just because, well, we needed a demonstration, and you know, dental hygiene is extremely important.

-I didn't see anything, said one of the investors.

-Didn't you? said Billy.

-No.

-Exactly. Now imagine you go to this site three or four times a day. And you get exactly the same message, reinforced at the subsensory level.

-What message?

-Exactly. That's the beauty of Pandemonium. Ipso facto.

-I don't think that's how you use "ipso facto."

-Hey, where have I seen you before? asked another investor.

-I don't know, said Billy. -Do you go to the Whole Foods on Fairfax?

-No.

-Oh! I know, said another of the investors. -You're the mountain lion–fighting guy.

-Umm . . . said Billy.

-That's right! It was on YouTube. Extremely awesome.

-I don't really like to be pigeonholed . . . I mean, did I fight a mountain lion? Yes. I did fight a mountain lion.

-This guy fought a mountain lion?

-Do you even watch YouTube? It was only the most popular video for three weeks straight.

-Someone from IT put a block on YouTube at my workstation. I think he was pissed because I made fun of his hair.

-Are you talking about that guy Roger? He's kind of creepy.

-Anyway . . . said Billy. -About Pandemonium.

-How on earth did you survive a fight with a mountain lion?

-I . . . uh . . . mostly I just threw clumps of dirt at it and stuff. I don't remember much of what happened, to be honest.

-That's right! You fell over and knocked yourself out on a big rock right before the end.

-That was the best part. I almost fell out of my chair. The mountain lion came over, pawed at you a little, then just trotted off. Maybe he thought you were dead.

–I always just assumed it was a fake, chimed in another investor.

–I can assure you it wasn't fake, said Billy, rolling up his sleeve. –I've still got a scar . . .

–Whoa. Dude, that is seriously gross.

–You know, we could use this, said one of the older investors.

–How do you mean? said Billy, unrolling his sleeve.

–This . . . fake Internet advertising thing. I mean, maybe it works, maybe it doesn't.

–I've got charts . . .

–Everybody has charts, son. But what everybody doesn't have is the guy who fought a mountain lion. That represents something.

–It does?

–Tenacity. Courage. Survival instinct.

–Hey, said Billy. –I recognize you from somewhere. Don't I?

He pointed at one of the other investors, an attractive redhaired woman in sober business attire.

–I can't imagine where, she protested.

–You're in the Moped Marauders, said Billy. –In fact, you're like the leader of the Moped Marauders!

–Julia? said one of the others. –What's he talking about.

–I really have no idea . . .

–You do ride a moped around Los Angeles, pointed out one of the investors. –Last time I was down there you drove up on it.

–It's not a moped. It's a Vespa.

–What's the difference?

–Is it light green? asked Billy. –I mean to say, is it tourmaline? And you have a matching helmet?

-How does he know that? Julia, how would the mountain lion guy know that?

-My name's Billy.

-Look, what I do on my downtime is not really anyone's business . . .

-It *is* you! exclaimed Billy. -You guys surrounded my car once.

-We don't do that, said Julia flatly. -We only go after the Critical Mass crowd. Bicycles, she added, for the benefit of the others. -They're like these crazed fascists who want to take over the streets for bikes. Bikes!

-I had dogs tied to my bumper.

-You're *that* guy?

-I don't even want to know why he had dogs tied to his bumper.

-I bet we can find it on YouTube.

-Can I make a sort of confession? said Billy. -I always thought you were really . . . well, I sort of have a crush on you. As a Moped Marauder.

-Really?

-So your name is Julia?

-Julia Fractal.

-That's your real name?

-Why wouldn't it be my real name?

-No reason.

-Were you ever in that bar on Fairfax across from Cantor's?

-I'm rarely *not* in that bar, said Billy.

-You and your friend did some kind of mind reading trick on me and a friend. Mostly the friend. I wasn't really buying it, but I couldn't figure out the trick.

-I'm sworn to secrecy on that, sorry.

-What if I said I'd go to dinner with you?
-Here's how it works, said Billy.

38. THE MIND READING TRICK EXPLAINED IN FULL, ALBEIT RELUCTANTLY, SITTING IN THE BAR THREE DAYS BEFORE THE KOREAN CHECK-CASHING FIASCO

See what I'm saying? said Billy, staring straight ahead. He held his hands outstretched across the booth toward Guy, who sat with his head in his hands, head down, eyes closed.

-I am, replied Guy.

Billy snapped his fingers three times.

-That's some kind of code, said the drunk girl who'd come over to join them, accompanied by a less-drunk friend. The less-drunk friend had red hair, and was very slim. She wore a light-green T-shirt decorated with sequins that spelled out a word. In the gloom of the bar it was difficult to make out the word. On the floor next to her seat was a helmet of some kind that matched the color of her shirt. Her friend, an artificial blonde, had on a black dress.

-No it's not a code, said Billy. -It's part of what Madam Rose taught us, it helps concentrate the mind. We can do it without the snapping but it's more difficult. Up to you . . .

-Let them snap, said the blonde, pushing the straw in

her almost-empty glass to and fro with the tip of her nose.

-Go! said Billy, throwing his hands theatrically toward Guy, who nodded gravely in response.

-I'm starting to get something, said Guy.

Billy snapped his fingers quickly five times.

-Tell me what you see! he commanded.

-I'm picturing a rock band, began Guy.

-Oh my God, exclaimed the blond girl. -This is creepy!

-There's some trick to it, insisted the redhead.

-Where is it? asked Billy.

-That's the strange thing. It's out in the desert some-where. It's like just this lone rock band standing out in the desert.

-Okay, said Billy.

-But it's not the band. You're picturing something, or rather someone, more specific. Guy rocked back and forth in his seat, in a sign of intense effort.

-Is it . . . he continued. -I'm getting a very clear picture now. Is it Bono from U2?

The blonde squealed in a mixture of delight and concern.

-No way! said the redhead.

-Did I get it right? Guy asked Billy innocently, looking around as if resurfacing from a trance.

Billy watched the skeptical expression on the redhead's face with more than usual attention.

-Do I know you from somewhere? he asked her.

-Almost certainly not, she replied. -But you're the psy-chic. You tell me.

-It doesn't work that way, murmured Billy.

★ ★ ★

SPOILER ALERT: The following paragraphs contain spoilers about the mind reading trick. If you don't wish to have your ability to believe in anything or anyone ever again completely trashed forever, we suggest you read no further from this chapter, or in fact from any other chapter of any other book containing fiction. Or just to be safe, any book whatsoever.

The first and most important element of the trick is alcohol. The second most important element is girls. The trick will work on guys, but they will be much less willing to admit it. They will go to all sorts of lengths to prove that the trick is in fact a trick and not a genuine display of extrasensory abilities. They will fail, because the secret of the trick is so absolutely, completely simple and banal that no one has ever successfully guessed the trick that does not already know the trick. The trick will also still work without alcohol, but it's less fun and therefore rarely performed sober or on sober people. One time Guy and Billy ended up at a dinner party where the assembled guests were so confounded they made Guy and Billy sit back to back facing away from each other, which of course had no effect whatsoever on the efficacy of the trick.

Here's how it works: the transmitter, in this case Billy, receives "something that can be pictured" from one of the girls, something concrete—at least at first, until a certain suspension of disbelief has been achieved by repeated success (and the occasional deliberate or even accidental failure, which only serves to underline the authenticity of the trick, because a trick cannot fail, but a genuine ESP transmission might be expected to fail for any number of reasons), at which point the girls or guys are free to suggest abstract concepts, people neither Guy nor Billy know but the girls or guys know, the make and model and color of the guys' or girls' friend's car, etcetera.

To heighten credulity, the receiver, in this case Guy, usually leaves the table and goes either outside or at least out of sight of the others, returning only when some-one—not Billy, obviously, that would be ridiculous—fetches him. In the meantime, the girl, because let's use as an example the one already presented above, has whispered into Billy's ear, "Bono." You'd be surprised how many times this is the first famous person that comes into the mind of anyone playing the mind reading trick. Billy nods, sagely, tells the girl, "Good choice. It's difficult, but I think I can picture him. Don't be disappointed if Guy doesn't get it, though, it's not an easy pick and the noise in this bar is very distracting."

It's always important to emphasize the distracting na-ture of the environment, in case, as has happened, some-thing goes drastically wrong and the trick repeatedly fails. This is why Guy and Billy will often reject the first few suggestions if they are judged to be too difficult to trans-mit, settling only when someone puts forward something assured of success. In this example, success was assured right away, which sometimes happens, happily.

Guy comes back in with a distracted air, sits opposite Billy, puts his head in his hands. Billy does a lot of preamble talking, to which Guy knows he doesn't have to pay atten-tion until Billy claps his hands together once, signaling the beginning of the actual transmission. "See what I'm say-ing," Billy begins, then snaps his fingers three times. "No, it's not a code," he assures the girls, which is actually part of the code. Then he does the theatrical "Go!" followed by five quick snaps. At this point Guy already knows that

Billy is transmitting the name of a singer, and is pretty sure he knows of which band, which means he already knows the answer. But Guy vamps, to add to the air of mystery, by claiming to picture a rock band. Billy slowly adds a couple more coded messages to draw out the tension, while Guy fills in imaginary details of the imaginary picture Billy is supposedly transmitting. Then, as if on the verge of passing out from the mental effort, he gives up the answer, to the astonishment of the girls, who immediately want to try again, and again, and Guy and Billy oblige, even switching from transmitter to receiver and back again with facility, never faltering and never letting on that the whole thing is an incredibly easy con.

The first letter of every sentence that Billy says is the code. In other words, when he says, "See what I'm saying?" the code is "S." Everything after that initial letter is meaningless, which is why it's easy to change around and avoid repetition that would give away the secret. The finger snaps are vowels: A, E, I, O, U, in that order, which is to say three snaps for I, which is what Billy did. So Guy understood at that point "S, I." Then Billy said, "No, it's not a code," etc., incorporating the code into his response to the girls—in other words, the third letter is "N." The theatrical "Go!" provided a "G," which led Guy to "sing," which he knew from long experience with Billy was shorthand for "singer," most likely, a fact confirmed when Billy snapped his fingers five times, indicating "U," at which point Guy understood the clue to be shorthand for "the singer of U2," and all the rest was stalling for effect.

39. MARCUS RECONSIDERS HIS LIFE AND COMES TO A PROBABLY UNSURPRISING CONCLUSION, TWO DAYS AFTER VISITING GUY AT THE HOSPITAL, A FEW DAYS AFTER THE KOREAN CHECK-CASHING FIASCO

Nothing good ever happens in the winter, thought Marcus, staring out the window of his Cambridge town house. Not one good thing. Christmas is a disaster, New Year's is a letdown, and now my dad's dead and my brother's right behind him. Guy was smart to stay in California. Winter never happens in Los Angeles. That must be the attraction, for most people. I mean, obviously that's the attraction, Endless Summer and whatnot, but besides that, when nothing good ever happens you don't notice as much, because there's the sun. There's the sea-blue sky. Is it going to be hot today, or merely comfortably warm?

I need the winter, though. I need the contrast of shadow and light to make sense of anything, not that I've done such a great job. Making sense. Mom's right, I'm not a very kind person. Nor am I a particularly honest person. I haven't been honest for years, not with my family, not with my wife, and least of all with myself.

Constance came into the room with a cup of coffee, which she handed to Marcus, wordlessly, smiling. He smiled back.

–I have to leave.

–Again? said Constance. –But you just got back. You've hardly had time to unpack.

–I know. But this is different.

Constance sat down with a quizzical look.

–What's wrong? she asked.

–Nothing. Everything. I feel like I'm moving backwards. Five gears in reverse, darling. Like the old soul song. That's all I've got. I'm always facing backwards. Benjamin's angel of history. I can only see what's happened, and look on in horror. I can never turn around.

–Because you're the angel of history.

–You know what I mean.

–Honestly, I don't. I usually do, but you've got me stumped, buster.

–Yeah. I've got myself stumped.

–Well, you've been through a lot in a very short period of time.

–I haven't, really. My dad went through a lot. My brother. Even my mom, because she actually loved them both. Loves. Whatever. I've just had to do a lot of responsible Marcus-type stuff. But if we're talking about emotional toll, which I think is what you meant, I really haven't. Maybe on some level that hasn't hit me yet . . .

–Marcus, if you're talking to me like this, which is pretty much the first time you've ever talked about anything to do with your family, in a serious way, then "on some level" is right here. On the surface.

–You're right. It's just that I don't feel it.

–What's "it"?

-Anything! Grief, anger, melancholy, sorrow, loss, pain.

-Those are good things not to feel, I'm thinking.

-That would be true. That would be true if the inverse were also . . . Are you happy Constance? Do you ever feel happy?

-No.

-No?

-Not really.

-Well, how is it I don't know this relatively important fact about you? I'm not happy either.

-I know.

-Jesus.

-I've never really thought of happiness as any kind of realistic goal.

-Really? Since when?

-Since forever. I don't remember the actual date and time of my epiphanies, dear. I'm not Joyce.

-Joyce who? Oh.

-So you want to leave? You think that will make things better?

-I don't know. I thought it was worth a shot.

-Have you . . . is there someone . . .

-What? Oh God, no. No. It has nothing to do with . . .

-I didn't think so. It's just one of the questions you're supposed to ask.

-And you? True to your name?

-More or less. Okay, more.

-You never liked my family.

-What's that supposed to mean?

-I don't know.

Constance sighed deeply. -No, I never did. In fact I couldn't stand your family. Except for your mom. I feel sorry for your mom. I didn't know that was an issue for you.

–It wasn't. It's not. You probably liked them better than I did. I couldn't think of anything else to say.

–Maybe there isn't anything left to say.

–Maybe there isn't. Shouldn't that make me feel sad?

–If you want my opinion, which is why you asked, I'm assuming, it's because you spend all your time feeling sad. You're so used to feeling sad that you don't know what it's like to feel anything else. Maybe you've even given up on the hope of ever feeling anything else.

–That sounds more like what *you* are feeling.

–Yes. Ironic.

–So what, then?

–What do you mean, what?

–I mean, what do we do now?

–I don't know. Until five minutes ago I didn't know that anything needed to be done.

–You mean you've been unhappy since I guess forever, and you were prepared just to keep on going, the way things are, indefinitely?

–Why not?

–Because ... this ... Marcus waved his hands around the room as a gesture to encompass his entire empty life.

–This?

–Isn't working. Isn't making you happy.

–It isn't making me unhappy. I can do that either with you or without you. I had the idea we were in this together. Why, what's your plan?

–I guess I don't have one.

–Remember way back before we got married, when we were both still dewy-eyed college kids, and you proposed to me, or however that went—you did propose, didn't you? We didn't just sit down and do a cost/benefit analysis of getting married . . . ?

-We might have. But that was after I proposed. And I was never dewy-eyed.

-Exactly my point. But one of the preconditions I insisted on imposing, I do remember this, specifically, was that if ever either of us wanted out, for any reason, he or she would be allowed to go. No muss, no fuss. I remember insisting because at the time I thought it would more likely be me who wanted out.

-You were right. At the time.

-If somewhere in the frozen tundra of your heart you believe that our marriage is the root cause of your . . . let's call it *dissatisfaction*, then you need to leave.

-I don't know what I believe. Either in the tundra of my heart or the fallow field of my brain.

-I don't think people like you and me are made for happiness, Marcus. I don't think we're constructed properly. We get along. We do things the right way. In order to be happy you have to be like Guy.

-Who you hate.

-He never brushes his teeth!

-I know. It's gross. But maybe sometimes you have to look beyond dental hygiene.

-Maybe I just did.

-But how can he be happy when he's comatose?

-Before the coma. Or maybe even after the coma, who knows? But it's the risks, the carelessness, the more or less complete lack of self-consciousness that allowed Guy to experience, I suspect, at least a few brief moments of happiness in his life. Along with a great deal of fear, and misery, and self-loathing, possibly related to tooth decay. That's something we don't have to deal with as much.

–I'm pretty good at the self-loathing.

–Yeah, but it's different. It's muted or muffled by your internal engine.

–I could get hit by a bus any minute now.

–People like us don't get hit by buses. We look both ways before crossing the street. And then we look again, just to be sure. We don't get the highs, but we don't get the lows, either. All we get is a kind of general malaise.

–World Fever. That's what Guy called it. He was convinced that the world was actually diseased, or at least the human race. He said World Fever would eventually cause the breakdown of ordinary life. He was really looking forward to that day.

–He may well live to see it. But I don't think World Fever's fatal, I really don't. I think it's like any other kind of fever, you just feel like shit for a couple of weeks, maybe you take some time off work, maybe you dose yourself with antibiotics and cold medicine and tough it out, but it goes away, eventually. After a while you forget you were even sick.

–But if everyone got sick . . .

–Then everyone would have to forget that they'd been sick. It sounds like a lot to ask, but when you think about the stuff we're used to forgetting on a daily basis . . .

–Yeah. You know, we never talk like this anymore.

–That's not true. We've *never* talked like this. Ever.

–Not even back in the dewy-eyed years?

–We were too stupid to talk about anything real back then. We thought the future was bright with promise. We had hope.

-I miss hope.

-I don't. It raises expectations, which are inevitably thwarted, and next thing you know your husband wants to leave.

-You knew I wasn't leaving.

-I knew you were unlikely to leave. I also knew you were likely to do something, maybe for the first time in your life, completely foolish if I didn't step in.

-Which is when you brought me coffee, said Marcus, staring into his now-cold cup. -Which I don't drink.

-You're welcome, said Constance, smiling, as she got up to leave.

-I have to do something, said Marcus, toward Constance's retreating form. -I have to make some kind of change. Otherwise . . . otherwise this has all been for nothing.

Marcus sat silently for a while, thinking.

-Maybe . . . maybe my antipathy toward wallpaper, I mean any kind of wallpaper, in general, is misplaced. Maybe there's something to wallpaper after all. Maybe there's good wallpaper and bad wallpaper, and I need to figure out the difference.

He looked, as if for the first time, around the wallpapered room.

-I mean, this pattern isn't so bad. Maybe in a different color . . .

40. UNORIGINAL OBSERVATION BY GUY FORGET ON THE FUTURE OF THE HUMAN RACE, INSERTED BY THE NOT ENTIRELY OMNISCIENT NARRATOR AT THIS POINT BECAUSE IT'S ABOUT TIME

Everyone—this is not, by the way, an original observation—is at his or her wit's end. Everyone has reached his breaking point, and passed that point without breaking. Stretched like a snare across a hollow drum, filled with miserable air. Hit it once, the world shatters.

That's what Guy thought, anyway. That was his guiding precept: the inherent frangibility of everything. Starting from that precept, Guy asked himself something: *How can this be good for me? How can I profit from World Fever?*

There's very little doubt the world is suffering from some kind of disease. From up close, it can look like a lot of little diseases, but when you take the long view, and Guy Forget always and ever only took the long view, to his credit, it's clear there's only one real disease. All the little ones are just variants, like different shades of the same kind of blue jeans. And you might as well call that macro-sickness World Fever, because everyone understands what it's like to have a fever, and most people have enough imagination to apply that understanding to the world in general. The world feels like hell. The world wants nothing more than to lie in bed and watch TV for a solid week, but there's no chance, because there are too many things that absolutely need doing. Things that *cannot* be put off. Besides, it's not a really bad, untenable, can't-even-function kind of fever, it's low-grade, where you feel stupid even complaining about being sick, because compared to people who really are sick, you're not sick at all. Stop being such a whiner. Get back to work. Take a couple aspirin, maybe one of those gel-caps that claim to push back inside your body all the worst symptoms, and *get back to work, World*.

You do that, though, I mean you do that for an extended period of time, where you don't really ever get enough sleep and you keep slogging away at your boring and pointless job (and there is nothing more boring and pointless than being the World, as Guy would often take pains to point out), and eventually shit catches up with you and you get really, really sick, or you just get really, really sick of being sick, and you crash. Not the solid week of bed and TV crash, either—the month or two of soul-crushing depression for no discernible reason crash, where you alienate your friends, probably lose your job, and eventually, because you can't think of any other way out and you're old enough to know that self-medicating via substance abuse is not a workable solution, you go on some kind of anti-whatever medication, which lifts you up just enough to function, to beg forgiveness from your friends, who say "Sure," but things are never really the same, and plead with your boss for your old job back, which either doesn't happen and you have to find a new one that turns out to be worse and pays less, or happens but now you're the prodigal worker and everyone treats you like dirt and you have to accept less pay too, as a condition for rehiring.

Guy was waiting, with whatever modicum of patience he possessed, not a lot, for that definitive crash. Not just waiting: preparing. His immediate plans might not have depended on the crash, but his long-term plans hinged like the gate to a mighty fortress on the coming collapse.

41. THE DAY GUY FORGET APOLOGIZED, WHICH IS ALSO THE DAY OF THE KOREAN CHECK-CASHING FIASCO, IN FACT NOT MORE THAN FIFTEEN MINUTES AFTERWARDS, ROUGHLY

I said I was sorry.
-It was the way you said it.

-What's wrong with the way I said it?

-Mainly, I didn't believe you.

-How's that my fault?

-Because of all the other times you said you were sorry but you didn't mean it.

-That's a really negative way to go through life.

-What is?

-I mean, I'm sorry. I said I was sorry. Nothing else I can say will help. I should never have called you a . . . well, it's no good repeating it, is it? The more you say, "A duck shits out more brains in five seconds than you'll ever hold in your peanut-sized cerebellum," the worse it sounds.

-You said a *baby* duck.

-Again. This is rehashing the past. Let's move forward.

-It'd be easier to move forward if I didn't have that mental image in my head. It's not very pleasant.

-You think the guys at Anzio had pleasant images in their heads when they fought their way inland? They had hellish images in their heads. Body parts blown off their good buddies. Brains splattered on their sleeves. That's just . . . I mean, how do you move past something like that? But they did. They moved past it. And so can you.

-What's Anzio?

-It was in a movie. I don't know. Some storming-the-beach thing. You know: war is hell.

-But we're not at war.

-We're not at war? You don't watch the news? Or do you mean just you and me—we're not at war with each other. That's true. But the country, the United States of these Americas, we are most definitely at war, buster, and if you don't get that, then you are as bad as a hippy, and possibly worse.

-It's not like a real war. Like World War Two or the War of the Roses.

-Which was a very entertaining movie, but I do see your point. You're saying it's not a real war unless there's a draft. Unless the children of privilege are sent to fight, no war can be considered true.

-I don't know what I'm saying. Sometimes I feel like you put words in my mouth even when I say the words.

-Trust me, if I were going to put words in your mouth, I'd put better words.

-Exactly what I'm talking about.

-You're right, that was uncalled for. Or maybe it was called for, but I should have not answered the call.

-Can we just get on with the . . . with whatever you have planned next?

-Here's the problem, Billy. I didn't really plan for next.

-Don't tease me, bro.

-You know how much I hate when you call me "bro." Or when you call anyone "bro." Or when anyone calls anyone "bro." Even ironically. Charlie did the same thing earlier. I don't know what made me angrier, him calling me "bro" or him screwing up a plan that we were nice enough to name after him.

-Sorry.

-But I'm not teasing you. I made no contingency for this sort of thing. I did not expect we'd end up on top of a hill with no money and the cops probably looking for us. In a stolen car.

-You don't know that it's stolen.

-I have a pretty good notion. I got it from Sven, and Sven didn't show. He's either in league with Charlie, or just a flake. Either way: stolen car. Though I must say, if you're going to steal a car, a Mini Cooper is not a bad choice.

-When you say no money, you mean not that much money. We've still got the one drawer's worth. That's like twelve grand, right?

-It is, or should be nearly exactly twelve grand. Which is exactly, or nearly, the same as no money. If I don't have fifty grand, I don't have anything.

-I'm just saying. As a contingency. We get six thousand dollars apiece, which is enough to probably get out of town and wait till things cool off.

-Billy. I'd tell you that I love you like a brother except I don't like my brother very much, so in fact I love you more than like a brother, or better than, you get the idea. But things are not going to "cool off." I don't even know what that means, "cool off." We bungled a burglary. We are on the run from the law, and we will always be on the run from the law.

-Always?

-Well, for a while. Until things cool off.

-You're a fucking chimp.

-Don't touch me.

-I said don't fucking touch me. What part of "don't fucking touch me" did you . . .

42. GUY TALKS TO VIOLET ABOUT FRIENDSHIP, LOVE, AND THE INTERCONNECTIVITY OF ALL THINGS, AND ENDS BY MAKING A POINT ABOUT THE IMPERMANENCE AND FRAILTY OF ALL HUMAN BONDS, SITTING ON HER BED THE ONE TIME HE WAS ALLOWED TO VISIT HER APARTMENT, FIVE DAYS BEFORE THE KOREAN CHECK-CASHING FIASCO

How long have we known each other, Violet?

–I don't know. Three weeks?

–Almost five months. Do you know how long five months is in friend slash lover years?

–Three weeks?

–It's like Krazy Glue years. Permanent. We're bonded together and nothing on earth or in heaven can ever separate us.

–I gotta go. By which I mean you should leave. Now.

–See you.

43. GUY TELLS BILLY THE STORY OF PANTHERZ, SITTING IN THE BAR WAITING FRUITLESSLY FOR THE ARRIVAL OF GREGORY TO DISCUSS HIS ROLE AS GETAWAY DRIVER, FOUR DAYS BEFORE THE KOREAN CHECK-CASHING FIASCO

Did I ever tell you the story about my friend's band? It's a good story. Well, it's not really a good story, in fact it's kind of a sad story and it doesn't even have an ending, but there are good parts of the story.

–When did you ever know someone in a band?

–Years ago. Back in Dayton. It was just these four guys from Peeper's Hollow, guys I knew from grade school. The singer was a jock but the guys in the band were freaks. When they started out they were really bad, and they had a really stupid name: Pantherz, with a "z." They'd play around town and nobody liked 'em, not even their family or friends. So they stopped. For like five years, they just disappeared.

–What happened?

–I told you: nothing. They just stopped. They didn't quit, or make any big pronouncements about quitting, and every once in a while you'd see someone from the band out at the grocery store or the gas station, so it's not like they disappeared as people. They disappeared as a band.

And then one day they came back. But they weren't called Pantherz with a "z" anymore. They were called King Shit and the Golden Boys, and they were unbelievably great. They played a show at a local bar, I think they opened for Horned Infirmary, it was at . . . I want to say the Rock Lodge, but I don't really remember, anyway it doesn't exist anymore so what's the difference? Place down in the Oregon District. Absolutely blew my mind. I'd never seen or heard anything that musically powerful before, or since. It was like they'd made some kind of Robert Johnson deal.

–But no.

–But no, they'd just spent five years practicing, getting really good, and writing much, much better songs. The lead guy, King Shit, obviously that wasn't his real name, I never did know his real name except that people called him William, jumped around onstage like a madman and sang like a madman about just crazy stuff, like, "I am heaven's circus act," or whatever. They had a song called "Liars in Motion," but I wouldn't have known this if the singer hadn't announced every title before starting the song. Except "starting the song" sounds tame compared to what these guys did. They *hurled* themselves at their songs, clattered through them like wild horses. Like they were desperate to get to the next song, and the one after that, because every song was better than the last.

–So then they got big?

–That's the weird thing. Still nobody in town liked them. I didn't understand that at first. I think maybe it's hard for people in a small town to embrace unmediated greatness. It's just hard to accept that these four guys, who look just like you and talk just like you and maybe you even know some of them or went to school with them, are any good. The argument being, I guess, well, if they're so great how come they're playing the Rock Lodge and not Scarlet Arena and how come they don't have a record deal and I don't hear them on the radio? If none of these things are true then it follows that they can't be any good. Because I found out—I actually did some research on this, I was mystified why nobody liked this band—that most people are willfully tin-eared with respect to music of any kind.

–Okay, then, what happened?

–They left town, of course. Went on the road. Started playing shows everywhere but in town, and the strange thing about that is when you go to New York City, for instance, from a small Midwest town, all of a sudden you're exotic, and therefore more interesting to a New York audience than a New York band would be. So you take exotic plus insanely great, which is a highly rare combination, and add a narrative, like, "How come we've never heard of these guys before, and did you know they never play out but just sit around in a basement drinking and playing music," which adds a patina of authenticity to the band ... People in New York are desperately hungry for something, anything authentic—for a really real experience—you wouldn't believe it, and you also wouldn't believe how hard it is to find authenticity in New York, which is the second most artificial city in the country after here. Whereas in the Midwest it's hard to be anything other than what you are. In fact, it's ridiculous to be anything other than what you are, despite which some people try, which is never pretty. The upshot being, King Shit and the Golden Boys are lionized in Gotham. Everyone loves them. Everyone is totally blown away. They sign a record deal within weeks, journalists fly in from London to interview them, celebrities come backstage to their shows. Everything changes. Until they return home, where nothing has changed. It's not like word travels along some kind of jungle telegraph about an obscure band from the Midwest that achieves sudden success. There's no way for the people in the band's hometown to know that anything's changed except that, well, they went out of town for a couple of weeks, which nobody would even notice because, as I said, even when the band was still called Pantherz nobody gave them much thought or noticed them. Noticed them particularly, is what I mean.

–I can imagine that would have been disappointing for them.

–More than just disappointing. It crystallized William's attitude toward his hometown, which had always been ambiguous, and now became fairly schizoid. He hated traveling, he hated leaving town, because he'd spent most of his life there and he felt comfortable there, much as he grumbled about the lack of respect and recognition. But he absolutely despised his fellow citizens. He laughed at them, but it was a bitter, scornful laugh. Years of resentment were thinly disguised by that laughter. And therein lay the problem.

–What do you mean?

–The seeds of corruption had been sewn. King Shit and the Golden Boys faced a clear choice: they could try, and probably succeed, although just as probably fail, to become more and more successful in commercial terms, until they finally reached the point where the folks back home would understand, would recognize, the genius flowering in their own backyard. So to speak. Unfortunately, to reach that level of success, several kinds of compromise would be required—artistic compromise, you understand, not the good kind of compromise, where two political parties reach an agreement that's in the best interest of everyone. The nature of politics is compromise. The nature of art is . . . I don't know what the nature of art is. But it's not compromise.

–So what did they do?

–They compromised. And it didn't work, as it often doesn't work. And they regretted it, after a few years of increasingly futile effort. And they jettisoned the whole idea, retreated to the basement, and made a record detailing their experiences called *The Power of Suck*. A great record. Maybe the greatest record.

–I'd like to hear it.

–You can't. They destroyed every copy. There's only bootlegged demos in circulation among die-hard fans, the shadow of the real record's shadow.

–Why on earth . . .

–Because it was literally too good.

–That makes no sense.

–Probably not. That's what makes, or I guess made, King Shit and the Golden Boys great. The only authentic act you can take as an artist is to destroy your creation. Anything else, any public display, is vanity. Just vanity.

–So they're not around anymore?

–Oh, they're around. But not making music. That was the end of the line for them. But there's plenty more where they came from.

–Really?

–No. Or at least I doubt it.

–What's the point of that story, then? asked Billy.

-The point of any story is the story itself, answered Guy, signaling Lucy for another drink. -Anyone who looks for morals or lessons in stories is worse than a fool, he is a coward.

-Seriously.

-All you need is love, said Guy, smiling at Lucy, who smiled back.

44. GUY AND VIOLET AND BILLY AT A CHINATOWN ART GALLERY, ABOUT A MONTH BEFORE THE KOREAN CHECK-CASHING FIASCO

I can imagine very little that would be more depressing than this, thought Guy. Tiny one-room galleries on a single closed-off block in Chinatown with sculptures that look like giant dental impressions but on closer inspection turn out to be upside-down cathedrals in meticulously melted wax. In a Styrofoam cooler with ice is either Coca-Cola or Mexican beer. Some of the galleries have hired deejays who make the process of pretending to examine the art that much more difficult, because you can't even hear your little cutting remarks about how all the paintings seem kind of spermy, which normally you would mutter under your breath but now you'd have to shout into the beat-segmented air and possibly, if the room had weird acoustics or there was a sudden lull between headache-y tracks, your sotto voce would carry much farther than you had intended and you would cause yourself, your host, your friends, and yourself again (because all embarrassment rebounds doubly on itself) hot shame.

But this is where the drugs are, because artists, whatever else their faults, like to do drugs, and so this is where Violet wanted to come, and so this is where we are, and so this is where I am. I will try not to look at the art. Must not look at the art. That's how they get you.

–Doesn't this art seem kind of spermy? said Billy, offering Guy a Mexican beer.

–That's what I . . . Clearly you don't know anything about art, Billy. The use of color in this one, for example . . .

–When can we leave? I'm bored.

–When Violet's ready.

–I don't get what's so special about her.

–That means a lot to me, man. Thanks.

–She's pretty and all that stuff, but I don't see the difference. I don't see why you're all hung up on Violet as opposed to the last one . . . what was her name?

–It doesn't matter. I mean, her name was Fleur, she was a lovely girl, of course it matters what her name was, but it doesn't matter what you or anyone else thinks about Violet. The fact that you don't see what's special about her only raises her value in my eyes.

–So this is . . . like, serious?

–I don't know what that word means.

–Okay.

–Yes, I suppose that, theoretically speaking, if you had to use a word to describe my feelings about Violet, "serious" would be acceptable to me, though not exactly accurate. But acceptable.

–Why would you have to use a word?

–Sometimes I don't know why I bother, Billy.

–No, but why?

–That was my point in saying "if you had to use a word."

You don't have to use a word, and I'd prefer if we didn't use a word, in fact I'd go further and prefer that people in general used less words, but it seemed to me that you were insisting. So I acquiesced.

-For someone who doesn't want to use a lot of words, you sure use a lot of words.

-Sometimes the simplest way to say something is to say it. And sometimes it's not to say it. And sometimes it's to wonder what the fuck I'm doing standing here talking to you, holding a beer which you know I don't like, and won't drink, when I could be . . . Guy looked over to see Violet talking to a short Asian kid dressed in a blue oxford shirt and khakis.

-Could be? prompted Billy.

-Thinking . . . murmured Guy.

-Well, who's stopping you? said Billy.

-What?

-Who was that guy? asked Guy.

-Some Caltech nerd. He was explaining to me this abstruse Internet coding he's developed. Which, as you know, is the quickest way to my heart. I'm still kind of weak at the knees. Hold me.

-Internet coding? What's it do?

-It throws up all over you if you even mention those two words again.

-It. Do.

-God. You need to know when to switch off.

-Is there an after-party? Will there be drugs?

-There's always an after-party. And there's always drugs. That's how I lure you down here to look at the spermy art.

-I wish people would stop reading my mind.

-You should stop writing it down then.

-How much longer . . .

-. . . will I put up with you? Hard to say. Why don't you go get your car and we'll talk about it on the way to the dealer's apartment.

-You're talking about the art dealer, aren't you?

-Is there any other kind? asked Violet, smiling enigmatically in a way that Guy thought was absolutely unfair.

-Do you think the Caltech nerd will be there?

-I imagine so. He owns the gallery.

-I thought you said he was a Caltech nerd.

-He is. His family's got money. He just does this to meet girls, or try to meet girls, which doesn't seem to be going well, judging from the frustration evidenced in these paintings.

-He did these?

-Well, technically, you could say his computer did them. But since he programmed the computer . . . you know, conceptual art is not really my thing.

-Then why do you come?

-I enjoy watching you suffer, is one reason. And the look on Billy's face, you can't really put a price tag on that. Also, and this is really just an ancillary to the first two reasons, if I ever want a show of my own, I have to play the game.

-But you like playing the game.

Violet sighed. -Yeah. The tortured artist thing doesn't really suit me.

-Wouldn't it be cool if I wasn't such a loser and I could support you and maybe buy you a gallery of your own and you could just paint all day?

-I'd go nuts out of boredom. If you weren't such a loser I probably wouldn't even like you.

-That's the sweetest thing anyone's ever said to me.

-I mean it too.

-I know.

The after-party was somewhere downtown, in an old Art Deco building that had been turned into loft spaces in an attempt to renovate the hollow core at the heart of Los Angeles, an effort that so far was doing okay but not spectacularly well. Guy wandered aimlessly through the crowd of black-spectacled hipsters, wondering if he should get a pair of black specs, even though his vision was perfect. Maybe even better than perfect. Better at any rate than the mediocre red wine in his glass tumbler.

I don't understand the vogue for alternative wine glasses, thought Guy. Is there a reason for it or is it just a statement of "We are not grown up, we're only playing"? And how does that statement work, exactly? There are people here in their fifties making the same statement. At some point the thing you're pretending to be becomes the thing you are, otherwise you look ridiculous. Or you look ridiculous anyway but you don't care, or you look ridiculous but you don't know you look ridiculous. That might be where I fit. Wish I knew how exactly to look at myself through other people's eyes.

-Some people shouldn't be allowed to breed, said a voice beside Guy, which turned out to belong to the Caltech nerd slash gallery owner.

-Did you say breed or breathe? asked Guy.

-I . . .

-It doesn't matter. I agree with both statements. But

only if I get to choose. I hear you've developed some new kind of Internet coding?

-You heard that?

-I have lousy hearing. But my eyesight is very good.

-It's true. I don't think it has any practical application, but it's kind of fun.

-Did someone say something about fun? asked Billy, sidling up to Guy and the Caltech nerd.

-A different kind of fun, said Guy. He turned back to the Caltech nerd. -So what is it exactly?

-Well, in essence, I've developed a way using 4D quaternion Julia set fractals ...

-Julia Fractals! exclaimed Billy. -That would be a cool name for a punk rock singer. I mean, you know, a girl.

-Ignore my friend, said Guy. -He's out of his depth talking about anything except nineteenth-century Eastern European literature.

-Maybe it's not that interesting, demurred the nerd.

-No, don't say that, I won't hear it, it absolutely *is* interesting, said Guy.

-It's nothing much. It's a way to untraceably interfere with websites by planting subsensory messages that would be unknowingly viewed by anyone who visits. For instance, if you hated Republicans, you could go to a Republican site and plant a message that says, *Vote Democrat.*

-And that would work?

-It depends how often he or she visits the site, the refresh rate of his or her browser, individual flexibility with regard to core principles, and so on. But over time, yes, I think it would have some kind of effect. Not in a drastic way—I don't think you could change someone's political outlook merely by suggestion, but you could probably affect his or her self-esteem if you wanted.

–And they would have no idea.

–None whatsoever.

–I see what you're saying. There really isn't any kind of real world implementation I can imagine, but it sounds like really good fun. I don't suppose you'd have any interest . . . No, that would be imposing.

Billy walked away with a look of profound blankness on his face. Guy and the Caltech nerd watched him go with disinterest.

–What would be imposing?

–I'd really love to see how this thing works. I do some amateur dabbling in HTML myself . . .

–Oh, this has nothing to do with HTML. That would be far too easy to trace. This is like reverse-engineered HTML. I actually call the coding LMTH, but that's a kind of private joke. This involves . . .

–Quaternion Julia set fractals. Yes, I know. Let's just for the sake of argument say that I don't have any background in programming, or physics, or . . . math. Would there be a way to explain or even show someone like that how this works?

–In theory. But it takes a lot of computing power. I have to use the lab at Caltech to produce anything near satisfactory results.

–Wow. I would so like the chance to see that.

–What, the lab?

–Yes, of course, the lab, but also just the . . . process. Do you have a name for it or anything?

–No.

–Okay, well, do you have a name? Mine's Guy Forget.

-Oh. Sorry. I'm Sven. Sven Transvoort.

-That is in no way your real name.

-I was adopted.

-I don't have an excuse.

45. SIMILIA SIMILIBUS CURANTUR

Violet sat in the permanent twilight of Guy's hospital room, unmoving, for hours. The soft hum of machinery and footsteps padding in the corridor were the only sounds, so she could hear the steady, regulated breathing of whatever was assisting Guy, keeping him alive, in the strict sense, though Violet could sense no life in her lover, no life in the room.

At length, she continued reading from the slim hardcover book balanced on an arm of the chair in which she sat.

-*That you cannot know the terror in a word. That it will not be the worst you fear. That you bring to the last the first sign. That you choose what to disappear.*

She gently shut the book.

-*That you choose what to disappear,* she repeated softly. -That's a nice line, isn't it, Guy? It's not always true, maybe it's not even ever true for ordinary people, but it's hopeful.

She held the book up to his sightless eyes.

-The guy who wrote this book—my friend Jimmy, you don't know him, he's a writer . . . I mean, obviously. He wants me to paint a flower for the cover of the paperback edition. I don't know why, but he's a little weird. In a nice way. I mean that in a nice way. No one's ever trusted me . . . I mean trusted my painting . . . Which amounts to the same thing . . .

She trailed off, put the book back on the armrest, balanced precariously.

-It's called *Tempo*. The book, I mean. I'm probably going to do something for him, but not under my own name. I think one of the things I'm going to choose to disappear is Violet McKnight.

She sat unmoving for some few minutes longer.

-My poor Icarus, murmured Violet in the direction of Guy's unmoving body. -Melted wings, third-degree burns. This is why I never get involved. It was wrong of me to interfere with Plan Charlie. I didn't trust you. Or if I did, I didn't trust my own trust in you, if that makes sense. Christ.

She could not help herself.

-I have no tears left, you see, Guy, there's nothing. Her eyes glittered in the murk. Violet was lying; she was full of tears, she was at the moment a silo of tears, but she would not allow the seams to burst.

-I wanted to give you something in return for what you gave me: hope for hope, so to speak. And what I've ended up giving you is despair for despair, even if you're currently unaware of that despair. Which means I have to carry the double burden of our mutual hopelessness. I'm completely prepared to do that.

-I can't blame Sven. I created him. Or rather, I created

the circumstances that led to his actions. And here you are. And here I am.

-Pleasures of the flesh, believing those pleasures to be without consequence, or if with consequences that those consequences were benign . . . never, never, never, never, never. Again. A body can only harvest so much sorrow

-And still I will go on. Can you explain that to me, Guy? Can you explain why I continue to exist, in the face of all reason? But what should I do? Expiate my sins in a drastic rejection of the life of men? How would that help anyone but me? How is that anything but selfish?

-I confess my sins, of omission, of commission, I confess them all. I confess only because I know you can't hear me, or, if you can, it's on some level where consciousness cannot penetrate, whether by choice or by a quirk of divine construction that saves the human heart from the worst excesses of its tepid and unfulfilling desires. We are all weak. We are all monstrous.

-And here's the thing, Guy. Here's the reason I fell in love with you—and yes, I know, I never told you that I loved you, that I love you, because it's not in my nature to make dramatic proclamations, and further what good would it have done?—you would not have participated in the killing of anyone, ever. You would have stood up to any tyrant, and not even for the right reason, necessarily, but simply because you refused to take human cruelty seriously. That was your chief virtue—your profound lack of seriousness.

-I wanted to own that, to possess it, to somehow absorb the part of you that could laugh off any crisis, that seemed in fact to seek out crises in order to laugh in their faces. Does that put you on the side of the angels or the devil?

I honestly don't know. *He who seeks hard things will have it hard,* it says somewhere in the Bible, I think E-mail to Hebrews. Even people who die are granted some kind of finality to their story. Your story has no determinate end. That, to me, is the definition of tragedy. Aristotle might disagree, but he's dead, and his story ended long ago. Probably happily.

    –Should some miraculous recovery occur, I will never know. I am a ghost, darling. But I am a ghost who loved you, and I am a ghost who will always remain part of you, living or dead, the boundary line between which grows blurrier every day, if you ask me, which no one ever will.

    With that Violet fell silent. She rubbed her eyes with the thumb and forefinger of her left hand, because she was left-handed, which was something very few people knew, because very few people noticed anything about Violet except her remarkable beauty, which wasn't even fourth on the list of her best attributes. But Guy had noticed.

    A nurse crept in to check on Guy's machines.

    –I'm sorry, said the nurse. –I didn't mean to intrude.

    –You didn't intrude, replied Violet. –I'm the intruder. I'm leaving anyway. She got up, slipping the book into a large suede handbag at the foot of her chair,

    Anything you want me to tell him? asked the nurse. –In case he wakes up.

    –That's a really good question, said Violet, disappearing by degrees.

    –Tell him that I love him, she said, from the shadows. –Tell him that there is no cure for World Fever, and no need for a cure. That he should start brushing his teeth. That . . . you know what?

By this time Violet was no longer Violet but a silhouette, limned by the dim fluorescence of the hospital hall.

-Tell him goodbye, said the faint outline of Violet as she vanished.

46. GUY'S MOM COOKS AN IN-ORDINATE AMOUNT OF FOOD FOR NO ONE

H e'll be hungry when he wakes up, thought Laura. Those IV tubes can't be giving him much nourishment, he already looks too thin. And he will wake up, and he'll wake up soon, so I'd better have enough food. Good thing I convinced Robert to get that extra freezer for the basement. That will come in handy.

The kitchen was surrounded by pots and platters of either already cooked dishes or those in preparation for the oven or stove. The bounty overflowed the kitchen and had spilled to the dining room table, which was likewise covered in several Thanksgivings worth of turkey, mashed potatoes, squash, green beans, more turkey, ham (for those who don't like turkey, and Laura couldn't remember whether Guy did or didn't), and tofu for Violet, who Laura seemed to remember was a vegetarian.

My hands are burned and scarred, thought Laura as she pulled both a pumpkin pie and a cherry pie from the stove without the aid of oven mitts, hoping by causing herself physical pain that she would forget, even for a moment, the psychic scars of her double loss. But what is that compared to the pain poor Guy must be in, somewhere in the recess of his brain, or the pain I saw on Robert's face in his last dying moments?

I stayed married to a man I no longer loved, because after all who can love so well and for so long? That was my fault, not his. To the end, to his end, I think he loved me. In his way. Just like he loved Guy. In his way. He never treated me badly, he never abused me, he provided for me and for our children. He was, for all his faults, a good man. My children too. Marcus and Guy. I loved my children even when they disappointed me, or worse, ignored me, as if a mother's love was something that could be taken or put back like the mealy apples I choose not to buy at Meier's, because this is America and we do not have to buy mealy apples if we do not want them, although sometimes, of course, you do want mealy apples, for instance when you are making apple pie, they're better for baking. I should have made an apple pie too. Who doesn't love apple pie? With whipped cream or even better vanilla ice cream on top.

I've played by the rules and it's time the rules started playing me back. One does not lose both a husband and a son in the course of one day, far away from each other, for separate and unrelated reasons. Guy was not a soldier, he had not been sent to a war zone to die, thus preparing his mother for the inevitable news, which is no longer delivered by telegram as in movies, I'm quite sure, but I don't know how they do it these days. Maybe someone in a uniform still comes to your door, and you let them in, and perhaps he is accompanied by an Army psychologist, or better yet a grief counselor, which is very close to "consoler," but I was given no such consolation. In part because my son is not even dead, I have been denied the reality of his passing, and am left with the brutal fact of his vegetable body, which Marcus insists cannot grow, or think, or act, and that I should unplug the machinery that feeds his vital functions, but how can you ask a mother to do such a thing, especially now?

Marcus is not cruel, I shouldn't have said that. My one remaining link to the world, and I brush him off like a pesky fly. Does he really love me? Does anyone? Do I love myself? There are good things about both of us, Marcus and me, there are things worth saving, or at least preserving. I do hope he will come to his senses and stop looking for happiness in dark places.

I don't know if I have enough tinfoil to cover all these dishes. That's what happens when you don't plan ahead.

47. WHAT HAPPENED TO THE VILLAIN SVEN TRANSVOORT

Is anyone really wondering, I wonder? I mean, now that the reader understands that my role was perhaps more extensive than I had originally indicated. In your place— though I won't presume to think for you, that would be arrogant—I would certainly assume that if I, Sven Transvoort, possessed even a modicum of shame I would spend the rest of my life in hiding, atoning for my many sins. But that would not be true to my nature, you see. Or perhaps you already see. It's difficult divining the thoughts of a reader one has never met, and will most likely never meet: this is why most writers write to and for themselves, or more precisely for an ideal version of themselves, a reader capable of understanding all the abstruse allusions and hilariously funny personal jokes which no ordinary person could possibly appreciate. While I am new to the writing game, I do understand, I think, how this tendency accounts for the bitterness one unexpectedly encounters should one find oneself in the unfortunate position of talking to a writer at a cocktail party, for instance. Whatever the actual content of the conversation, the inevitable subtext is, "I'm not appreciated. I'm misunderstood. No one gets me. No one, not one reader, even the fanatics who send me articles of their intimate clothing, has ever approached the empyreal heights my prose dares them to climb, no one save myself has ever planted the flag of comprehension on the lofty peak of my mountainous accomplishment. And really, that was just a minor work, an aperitif. The storm brewing inside me, even as we speak about the rising cost of real estate here in Los Angeles, which has more significance than you, puny mortal, could possibly grasp, will rattle the gates of heaven with its wondrous insights, its lyric prose, and its consummately perfect form. And no one will ever know. Not for a hundred years after my death, when the shallow tides of popular culture have washed away the bitter taste of 'relevance,' will some enlightened scholar unearth my work, like a treasure trove of sea glass on a rocky beach in Maine, in summer, when the blackberries grow thick on thorny vines . . ."

And so on. Or maybe that's just me, maybe I'm the only one who thinks unreasonably high of himself, and the rest of the ink-stained wretches, to use the cliché currently in vogue, are filled with such self-loathing that the mere thought of whatever it is they last published fills them with shame, and horror, and what drives them to keep writing is the hope against hope that maybe, by some miracle, the next effort will rise above worthlessness to attain, at least, some kind of adequacy. These, I imagine, are the kind of writers who read their reviews, all of them, and who spend most of their days Googling themselves to see if some obscure weblog chronicler has chanced upon one of their books and written something not entirely unkind. Which not-entirely-unkind mention will be immediately discounted by a misquote, or an easily perceived complete failure to understand the point, the essence, the what-have-you of the book, whereupon our poor self-lothario plunges ever deeper into the slough of despond (*The Pilgrim's Progress*, citation needed).

To answer your original question, then, Sven: I *am* in hiding, and as you may have guessed, in a small North-eastern town that gives on the ocean, battered in winter by gales of an almost unimaginable force, but which I find somehow comforting: God's anger has a kind of majesty that nevertheless fails to touch me, or at least harm me. But I'm not in hiding out of guilt or shame or any of those writerly emotions described above. I'm in hiding, or perhaps more appropriately I have recused myself from the thrum of quotidian human affairs, because I do not like people, and people, in general, do not like me. The things I have done, while wider in scope than previously admitted, yes, I did because . . . for reasons that . . . well, if the reader requires any further explanation I would urge him (or her, I am no misogynist) to go back and consult my previous entries, all of which I stand by unreservedly. The Guy Forget episode remains for me, will always remain for me, an enchanting parenthesis. The root cause of my hatred may not be as rational as mere jealousy, but reason is overrated in the affairs of men. Or women. I hated Guy from the moment he walked out of the Smog Cutter, and later, still, into my gallery, and I resolved to destroy his life. To steal his girlfriend, to convince him that a bogus technology was the key to his future, and to watch in glee as he was arrested for a crime that he was driven to commit by his absolute conviction that he had stumbled upon a figurative goldmine. That I failed in all of these aims is, I think, not a failure of execution but a bad joke by the gods of chance. I also perhaps underestimated Violet's capacity to love, or at any rate to love Guy.

In any case, I win. My objective has been accomplished, and I am in the clear. The technology I pretended to show Guy that night at Caltech does not work, could not work, is not even physically possible. Any attempt by his idiot friend Billy to sell that technology will result in complete embarrassment, which to be honest is the best one can hope for a simpleton like him. Any further punishment would be gilding the lily. I would like to see his face when he presents his "invention" to the venture capitalists in Menlo Park, but we can't have everything we want, otherwise Violet would be here right now, filling my pipe, bringing me a sherry, stoking the fire in my hearth and my heart.

We can't have everything we want. Some people don't get anything they want. I have, at least, the satisfaction of partial satisfaction.

A funny thing. Today's my birthday, you know. I'd almost forgotten. I'd almost forgotten to celebrate. Because the birth of Sven Transvoort, adopted Taiwanese orphan, raised and then well provided for by two well-meaning but let's face it ultimately fatuous and condescending parents—I mention this only because no one knows my real birthday, and picking today, April 1 . . . I mean, that's not really very nice, is it?

At that moment a knock on the door. Who on earth, thought Sven, it's eight o'clock at night and I don't know anyone . . .

-Domino's Pizza! announced a voice from behind the heavy door, in answer to Sven's query.

Cautiously, he opened the door. -I didn't order . . .

-No sir, this was bought and paid for long distance. Said it was a birthday present. Very specific instructions.

-Who? How?

-Among these instructions there were several provisions insuring complete anonymity on the part of the purchaser.

-Are you by any chance studying . . .

-Second-year pre-law at Bangor College, sir.

-Okay. Sven reached into his pockets, came up empty. -I'm afraid . . .

-No gratuity will be necessary, sir. All that's been taken care of.

He accepted the pizza and closed the door. Set the box down on an ottoman and stared at it for perhaps five minutes, considering.

With one swift movement Sven reached over and flipped open the cardboard box. He froze. His eyes widened in fear, a position they would maintain for more or less the rest of his miserable existence.

48. BILLY VISITS GUY IN THE HOSPITAL WITH HIS NEW GIRLFRIEND, JULIA

-You should say hi at least. He's never met you.

-But he can't . . . Hi, Guy. I'm Julia.

-Isn't she great? You'll never believe, she's the girl I was telling you about, remember, the leader of the Moped Marauders? But she's also a venture capitalist in her spare time.

-More like the other way around.

-Anyway, where do I start? First of all, I took the money that was left to you, and therefore to me, and thanks for that, that was really very sweet, by your dad, and I had some guys cook up a beta thingy according to your specs—they kept telling me it was nonsense, there was no way it could work, but I had the money so they had to do what I said. Which is, I think, the first time in my life that's ever happened. Then I scheduled a meeting with a VC group up in San Francisco . . .

-Menlo Park.

-Whatever. And I showed them Pandemonium, and

they loved it! They're investing like five million into . . . into . . .

-Into a working company that we can then bring to market, finished Julia. -Initial estimates of our public of-fering, which is less than a month away, indicate that Billy is going to be worth somewhere between half and three-quarters of a billion dollars after the IPO.

-Yeah. Which is a hell of a lot of dough, and I owe it all to you. I want you to know, Guy, I'm going to set aside a substantial sum, like at least ten million, or at least five, or something, to try to find a cure for . . . comas, or whatever.

-I don't remember discussing . . .

-Hey, it's still my money, darling. At least until I make an honest woman of you. And also, Guy, I tracked down Violet. Which actually was a little hard, because she changed her name. And she's moved up to Portland. She's been going to art school and, well, I guess obviously, painting. Anyway, she was very happy to hear about the success of your idea, but she didn't want any part of your share of the money. She really looked good, though, Guy. I mean, she was always totally hot . . .

Julia eyed him disapprovingly.

-If you're into that superficial beauty thing. Not my type at all. But she looks healthy, Guy. I think she's quit all that junk you guys were taking. I thought you'd like to know that. She asked about you. I . . . I didn't really know what to say. I kind of couldn't say anything, you know how I get sometimes. Anyway, she smiled this kind of sad smile and nodded. I'd swear there were tears in her eyes, Guy. Well, maybe not tears, real tears, but she was close to tears. You know how when girls get close to tears, their eyes go really shiny? It was like that. I think that's a good sign, Guy. I think she really did like you. A lot. And I think that would mean a lot to you, is why I'm telling you.

-Oh! And I found out where Sven Transvoort is. That took a little more digging, but it's amazing what you can find out when you have money. Okay. I know you'd probably rather I have him, you know, killed or somehow crippled for life, but I'm a responsible guy now, I can't just think of myself, or at any rate think of myself thinking of you. So I decided it would be more fun, as well as more sort of psychologically terrifying, just to send him a pizza every year on his birthday, which by the way is April Fools' Day, how great is that? And on the pizza I have them spell out *EPIC FAIL*. This year I used pineapples, but I don't want to be limited by pineapples. I want to get creative with this shit.

-I wish you'd just report him to the police, said Julia.

-That's the thing about Sven. He was very slippery. There's no proof of his involvement in any stage of what happened. When Violet told me all that stuff, I couldn't believe it. But there's no way she'd come back here and testify, and otherwise there's no way we'd get a conviction. That's what my people say, anyway.

He turned back to Guy. -I think my way is more Guylike anyway, right?

-It's too bad he can't hear you.

-We don't know that. We don't know what he can and can't hear.

-Actually, we do, said Julia softly.

Billy pulled a laptop out of the bag at his side, went over closer to Guy's head, and booted up the computer.

-I wanted to show you this. First fruits of your labor, so

to speak. Here we have a typical sports website. Nothing out of the ordinary, at least at first. Until you look closer: no ads! No banners, no URLS saying, *Click here to win a football!* or whatever they usually say. Nothing. A completely ad-free site. Or so the visitor thinks. I programmed this one randomly, so even I don't know what the ad is really for. I'm telling you, I still have no idea if this thing actually works or not. I refreshed the site for like twelve hours in a row last week, and I haven't developed a craving for anything obvious.

–You started smoking, said Julia.

–I'm under a lot of pressure! And the smooth, rich taste of Camel Lights sacrifices none of the pleasure but cuts harmful tar and nicotine to almost negligible levels.

–What?

–What? My point is, Guy, the genius of your little invention is that no one will ever really know if it works or not. But they will pay, and they will continue to pay, and by the time enough scientific studies have been commissioned to decide whether or not it in fact does or doesn't work, well, if it works, wonderful, and if not, we'll still have the money. It's a . . . what do you call that, Julia?

–Win-win.

–Oh . . . oh . . . you never saw my YouTube. This is the thing that made everything else possible. For whatever reason, the guy in San Fran . . . Menlo Park, the head guy, was really impressed by this YouTube video of me fighting a mountain lion, which happened after you left me down at the bottom of that hill. Obviously I'm not angry about that, because if you hadn't, I would never have fought the mountain lion, and then . . . well, you know . . .

Billy clicked play on the YouTube video and the

sounds of the mountain lions growls intermingled with Billy's pathetic yelps.

As he watched, fat, clownish tears began to roll down Billy's cheeks.

–I wish you weren't in a coma, Guy. I wish you were still my best friend, laughing at my stupid mountain lion fight. If you were here, forget the money, the success, any of it, you would be rolling on the floor, literally rolling, with laughter. Nobody laughs like that anymore, Guy. I'm rich and successful and nobody dares laugh at me. It's awful. It's so, so awful.

Julia came over to Billy, gently held his shoulder with one hand, gently shut the lid on the laptop with the other.

–It's time to go, she whispered.

–Okay, said Billy, weakly, drying his face with the cuff of his expensive shirt. –Okay. Bye, Guy.

49. GUY FORGET ON THE CEILING

Why no one ever thinks to look up, thought Guy, floating six feet above his body in the hospital room. Suppose they wouldn't see me anyway. Suppose I'm invisible as air.

I can't hear them but I can see them. I can see Marcus and Mom, and I know they're talking about pulling the plug, or rather plugs, it's misleading to think there's only one plug, there's a whole bunch from what I can tell. I wish I could convey to them: It's okay, you can pull the plug, the thing in the bed is no longer me, it's a shell, an empty room, and I'm up here, on the ceiling, and every day that passes I get a little bit lighter and I float a little bit higher.

I saw Violet, for hours and hours. I saw Violet cry. I saw that Violet loves me, and blames herself, and that was the one time I was tempted to come down and reinvest my body once more just so I can tell her everything that happened was exactly the right thing, and that I'm ... well, I'm actually happy. I am, for the first time, and probably—though

I can't actually see the future, or can I?—will remain happy. For eternity. She'll understand, eventually. I'll make sure.

I saw Billy, and I can't believe he's actually going out with the Moped Marauder, who is by the way insanely cute, they make a perfect couple. I don't know what he was trying to tell me, but that video of him being attacked by a mountain lion? Oh my God, that was the single funniest thing I've ever seen in any of my lives.

Soon I'll float free of this room, and after that I have a choice. I can see the bright rupture above, and every fiber of my weightless being longs to head into that brightness, and the peace and calm that dwells there endlessly.

But before that, there's something I have to do. I have to pay a visit to an old friend. I have to go to Maine, or some version of Maine, I'm not really sure how this projection thing works, but I'll get it down. Unfinished business, you see. When I leave, I mean leave for good, I don't want anything tying me to this brutal plane of existence.

What I would tell those I love and have loved, what I would tell everyone who loves and has loved, what I would tell everyone: it's so very easy, you see. You've already solved the puzzle of being, you solved it the moment you opened your little baby eyes and saw a relatively out-of-focus version of someone who may or may not have been your mother smiling down at you. Everything else is a distraction. The only answer in this or any other world that matters is yes.

Also available from Akashic Books

ARTIFICIAL LIGHT
a novel by James Greer
338 pages, trade paperback original, $15.95
*Winner of a California Book Award Silver Medal for First Fiction; a
selection of Dennis Cooper's Little House on the Bowery series.

"Greer's prose shines [with] moments where the writing becomes
urgent and truly moving. This is the way the real and the invented
Kurt [Cobain] would have wanted it."
—*Los Angeles Times Book Review*

"Greer does a superb job of transcending conventional genrefication,
bringing something fresh to contemporary literature . . . A very
enjoyable read [with a] highly inventive structure, full of eccentricities
and rock music factoids . . ."
—*Library Journal*

HEADLESS
short stories by Benjamin Weissman
162 pages, trade paperback original, $12.95
*A selection of Dennis Cooper's Little House on the Bowery series.

"[A] playful mélange of erotic black comedy and domestic pathos,
dysfunctional families and all-too-functional men, dictators and
lumberjacks. Weissman is an expert juggler of tone . . ."
—*Los Angeles Times Book Review*

"Weissman is an impishly audacious writer, and that's reason enough
to love *Headless,* his new collection of short stories."
—*San Francisco Chronicle*

ALICE FANTASTIC
a novel by Maggie Estep
248 pages, trade paperback original, $15.95

"[T]he storytelling has vitality and a spirit of rebellion, giving us hope
for the future of all those bad girls with dirty faces."
—*New York Times Book Review*

"Few will be able to resist Estep's blend of barely controlled lunacy-
cum-pathos and reconciliation . . . If everything is cosmically
connected, then it's especially so in Estep's surreal, sad, and sweet
world, which is well worth a visit."
—*Booklist*

ADIOS MUCHACHOS
a novel by Daniel Chavarría; translated by Carlos Lopez
248 pages, trade paperback original, $13.95
*Winner of an Edgar Award

"Celebrated in Latin America for his noir detective fiction, Uruguayan author Chavarría makes his English-language debut with this fast-paced novel, set in Cuba ... Mixed together, these ingredients make a zesty Cuban paella of a novel that's impossible to put down. This is a great read, recommended ..."
—*Library Journal*

AMERICAN VISA
a novel by Juan de Recacoechea
translated by Adrian Althoff, 264 pages, trade paperback, $14.95

"Dark and quirky, a revealing excursion to a place over which 'the gringos' to the north always loom."
—*New York Times Book Review*

"Harrowing and hilarious." —*Boston Globe*

"A serious novel made palatable by humor as dry as the Andean uplands in which it is set." —*Kirkus Reviews*

THE DUPPY
a novel by Anthony C. Winkler
178 pages, trade paperback, $13.95

"Winkler has a fine ear for patois and dialogue, and a love of language that makes bawdy jokes crackle."
—*New Yorker*

"Winkler never glosses over Jamaican deprivation, prejudice, and violence, yet the love of language—and the language of love—somehow conquers all. It's almost as if P.G. Wodehouse had strolled into the world of Bob Marley ... Winkler's fiction magics the island into a place of rough-edged enchantment."
—*Independent* (UK)